DISNEY PRINCESS

Comic Strips Collection

JOE BOOKS LTD

Disney PRINCESS
Comic Strips Collection

Written by Amy Mebberson, Geoffrey Golden,
Patrick Storck, Georgia Ball, Pat Shand
Rainy Day story by Caleb Goellner
Illustrated by Amy Mebberson
Cover by Amy Mebberson
Lettered by AndWorld Design
Series Editors: Steffie Davis / Deanna McFadden
Amy Mebberson / Jesse Post
Design: Sayre Street Books

Thanks to: Gianfranco Cordara, Danny Saeva,
Eugene Paraszczuk, Carlotta Quattrocolo, Julie Dorris,
Roberto Santillo, Jean-Paul Orpinas,
Manny Mederos, Chris Troise

JOE BOOKS LTD

CEO: Jay Firestone
COO: Jody Colero
President: Steve Osgoode
Associate Publisher: Deanna McFadden
Executive Editor: Amy Weingartner
Production & Editorial Assistant: Steffie Davis
Sales & Marketing Assistant: Samantha Carr
Publishing Assistant: Emma Hambly

DISNEY PRINCESS COMIC STRIPS COLLECTION, September 2016. Published by Joe Books Ltd,
489 College Street, Suite 203, Toronto, Ontario, M6G 1A5. Copyright © 2016 Disney Enterprises,
Inc. All rights reserved. No portion of this publication may be reproduced or transmitted, in any
form or by any means, without the express written permission of the copyright holders. Names,
characters, places and incidents featured in this publication are either the product of the author's
imagination or are used fictitiously. Any resemblance to actual persons (living or dead), events,
institutions, or locales, without satiric intent, is coincidental. Joe Books™ is a trademark of Joe
Books Ltd. Joe Books® and the Joe Books logo are trademarks of Joe Books Ltd, registered in
various categories and countries. All rights reserved. Printed in Canada.

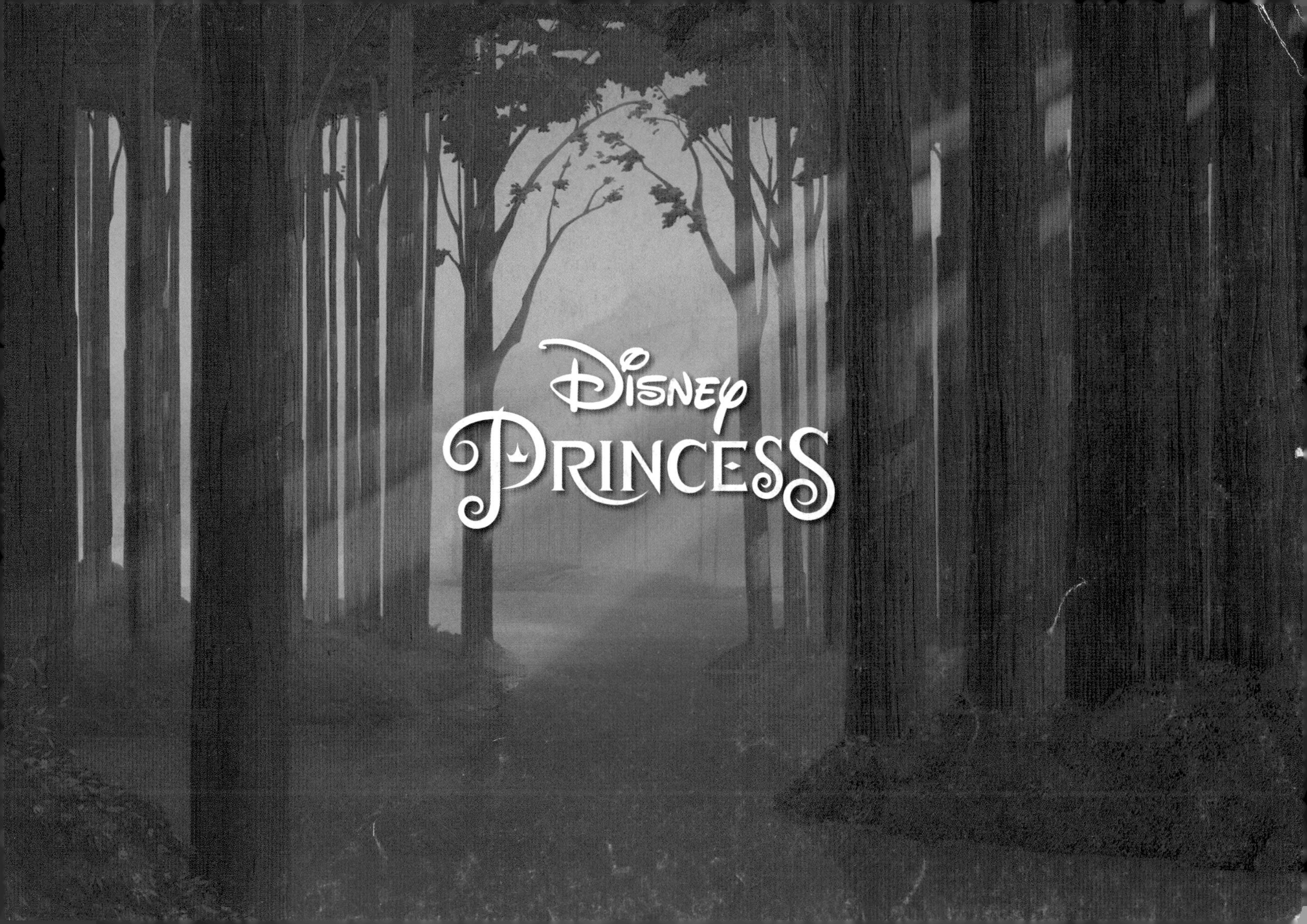
Disney
Princess

GASTON'S BOOK CLUB

I READ A BOOK ONCE!

REALLY? WHAT WAS IT ABOUT?

I'M NOT SURE...

DID IT HAVE WORDS?

I... THINK SO?

WAS THIS BOOK EVEN OPEN?

UM...

SO WHAT YOU'RE REALLY SAYING IS YOU SAT NEXT TO A BOOK ONCE, *MAYBE*.

STILL COUNTS!

End

WORLD OF RAIN

THIS NEVER GETS *OLD*, DOES IT?

ALADDIN, WE SHOULD GET BACK. I HEARD IT'S GOING TO--

SOARING THROUGH THE SKY, THE BREEZE WHIPPING THROUGH OUR HAIR. JUST YOU AND ME, SEEING THE--

PLIP

KRA-KOOM

HOW ABOUT YOU SHOW ME THE WORLD *ANOTHER* TIME?

End

SNEAKING

NOT SO LOUD, MERIDA! A LADY MOVES QUIETLY ABOUT THE CASTLE.

LATER...

I THOUGHT IT WAS A WEE BIT *TOO* QUIET...

End

BUCKETHEAD ONE

OH, PRINCE BUCKETHEAD? I HAVE A SURPRISE!

I HAVE A NEW HAT! IT MATCHES MY GOWN!

WELL, THERE'S NO NEED FOR *IMPERTINENCE*, SIR!

End

MEDITATION TRAINING

BOYS, I'VE BEEN THINKING WE MIGHT BE GETTING A BIT SOFT...

SOFT?!

WE HAVE ENJOYED THE SPOILS OF VICTORY. PEACE, HOME-COOKED MEALS, A COMFORTABLE PLACE TO REST.

MM, I *GUESS*...

IF EXPERIENCE HAS TAUGHT US ANYTHING, IT'S THAT WE NEED TO STAY SHARP, FOCUSED AND STRONG!

BUT A NAP AFTER A MEAL IS HOW I MEDITATE!

MEDITATION! THAT'S A GOOD START!

OR WE COULD BUILD A WALL TO DEFEND US. NOT A GREAT ONE, BUT DECENT.

TODAY WE WILL PRACTICE MEDITATION.

BREATHE AND FOCUS.

THE FIRST THING YOU MUST DO IS CLEAR YOUR HEAD OF ALL DISTRACTIONS.

NOT EVEN CLOSE.

I *AM* BREATHING!

GO INSIDE YOUR HEAD TO A CALMING MEMORY.

SOMEPLACE TRANQUIL, WHERE YOUR ENERGY CAN FLOW.

WHERE YOU CAN ESCAPE THE NOISE OF LIFE.

WHERE YOU CAN BE TRUE TO YOURSELF.

YOU WERE EXPECTING A TRANQUIL MEADOW?

OH, THEY'RE LEARNING CONCENTRATION! FOCUS.. SHEDDIN' DISTRACTIONS!

LET'S BUMP IT TO THE NEXT LEVEL!

MUSHU! MEDITATION ISN'T A CONTEST!

EXCUSE ME! WHEN CANNONS ARE GOING OFF ALL OVER AND YOU CAN FIND INNER PEACE...

...MAYBE YOU'LL REMEMBER WHO MADE YOU *GONG STRONG!*

DONK DONK DONK

HE HAS A POINT.

SEE? NOW LET'S GET *MEDITATING.* THIS IS *HEAVY!*

OKAY, LET'S GIVE THIS PEACE OF MIND A WHIRL.

AS I WAS SAYING, YOU MUST REMAIN QUIET IN ORDER TO FIND QUIET.

GOT IT!

THERE IS NO NEED TO RESPOND TO ANY EXTERNAL INFLUENCE.

ROGER THAT, 10-4! LOUD AND CLEAR!

BE QUIET!

SHOULD WE BE TAKING LESSONS FROM HER? SHE DOESN'T LOOK RELAXED *AT ALL!*

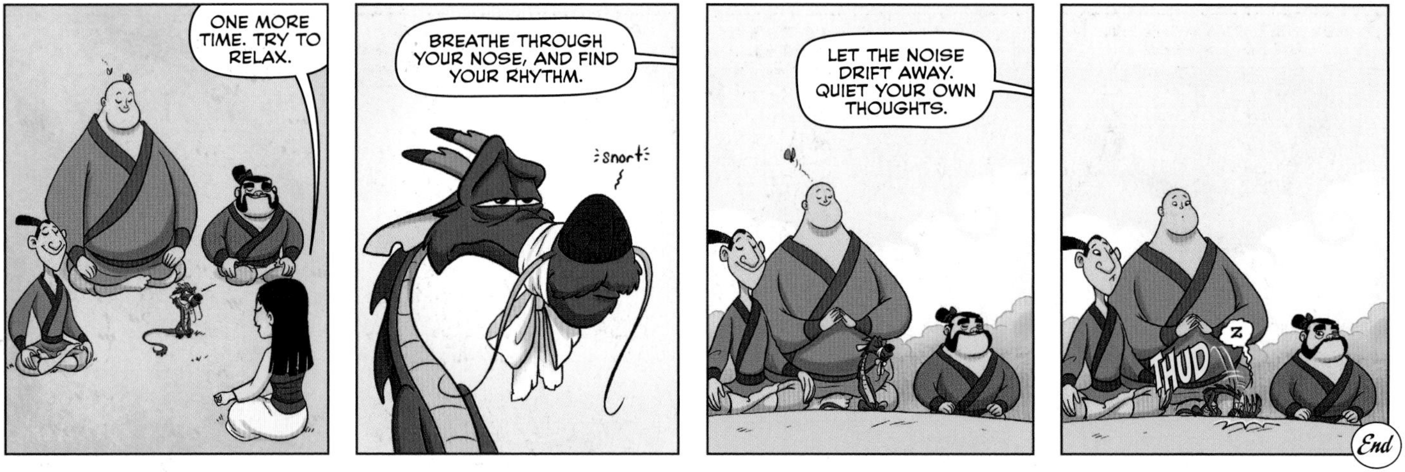
ONE MORE TIME. TRY TO RELAX.
BREATHE THROUGH YOUR NOSE, AND FIND YOUR RHYTHM.
snort
LET THE NOISE DRIFT AWAY. QUIET YOUR OWN THOUGHTS.
Z
THUD
End

HOW TO SLEEP

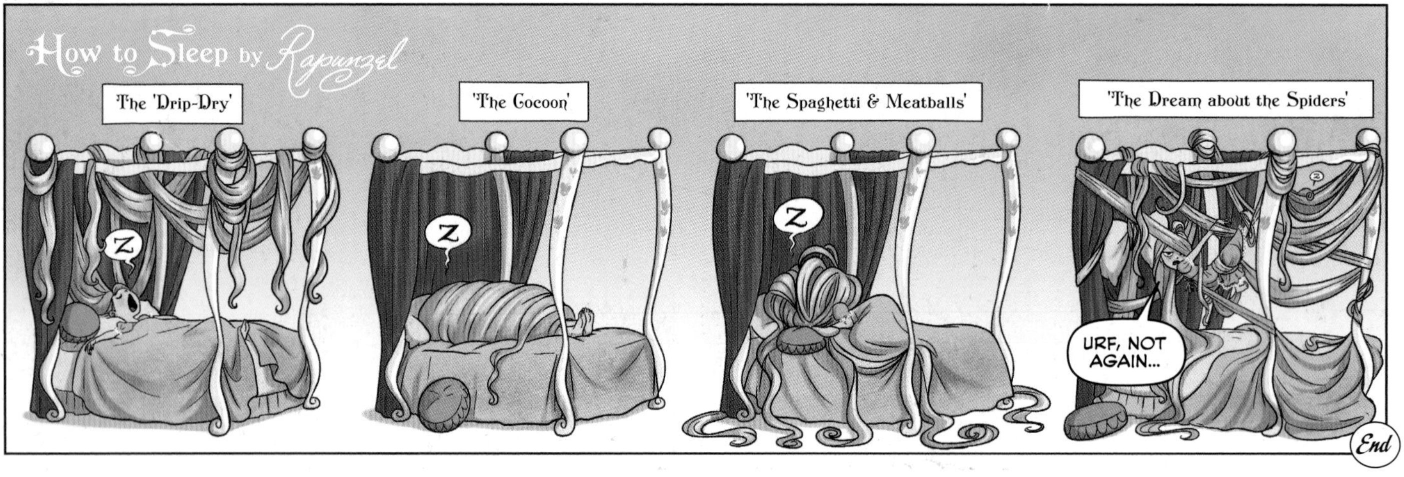
How to Sleep by Rapunzel
'The 'Drip-Dry'
'The Cocoon'
'The Spaghetti & Meatballs'
'The Dream about the Spiders'
Z
Z
Z
URF, NOT AGAIN...
End

MUSIC CLASS

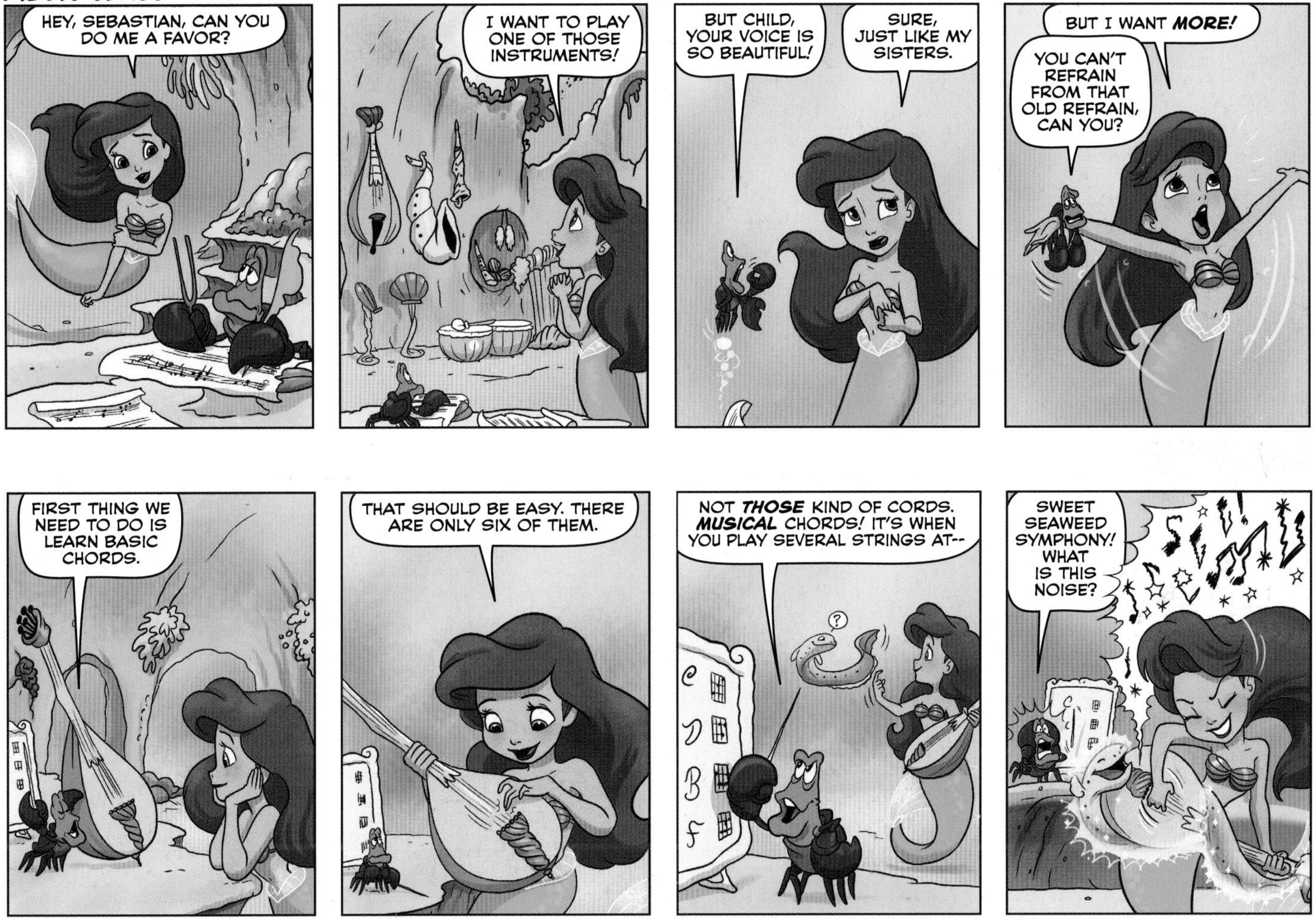
HEY, SEBASTIAN, CAN YOU DO ME A FAVOR?
I WANT TO PLAY ONE OF THOSE INSTRUMENTS!
BUT CHILD, YOUR VOICE IS SO BEAUTIFUL!
SURE, JUST LIKE MY SISTERS.
BUT I WANT MORE!
YOU CAN'T REFRAIN FROM THAT OLD REFRAIN, CAN YOU?
FIRST THING WE NEED TO DO IS LEARN BASIC CHORDS.
THAT SHOULD BE EASY. THERE ARE ONLY SIX OF THEM.
NOT THOSE KIND OF CORDS. MUSICAL CHORDS! IT'S WHEN YOU PLAY SEVERAL STRINGS AT--
SWEET SEAWEED SYMPHONY! WHAT IS THIS NOISE?

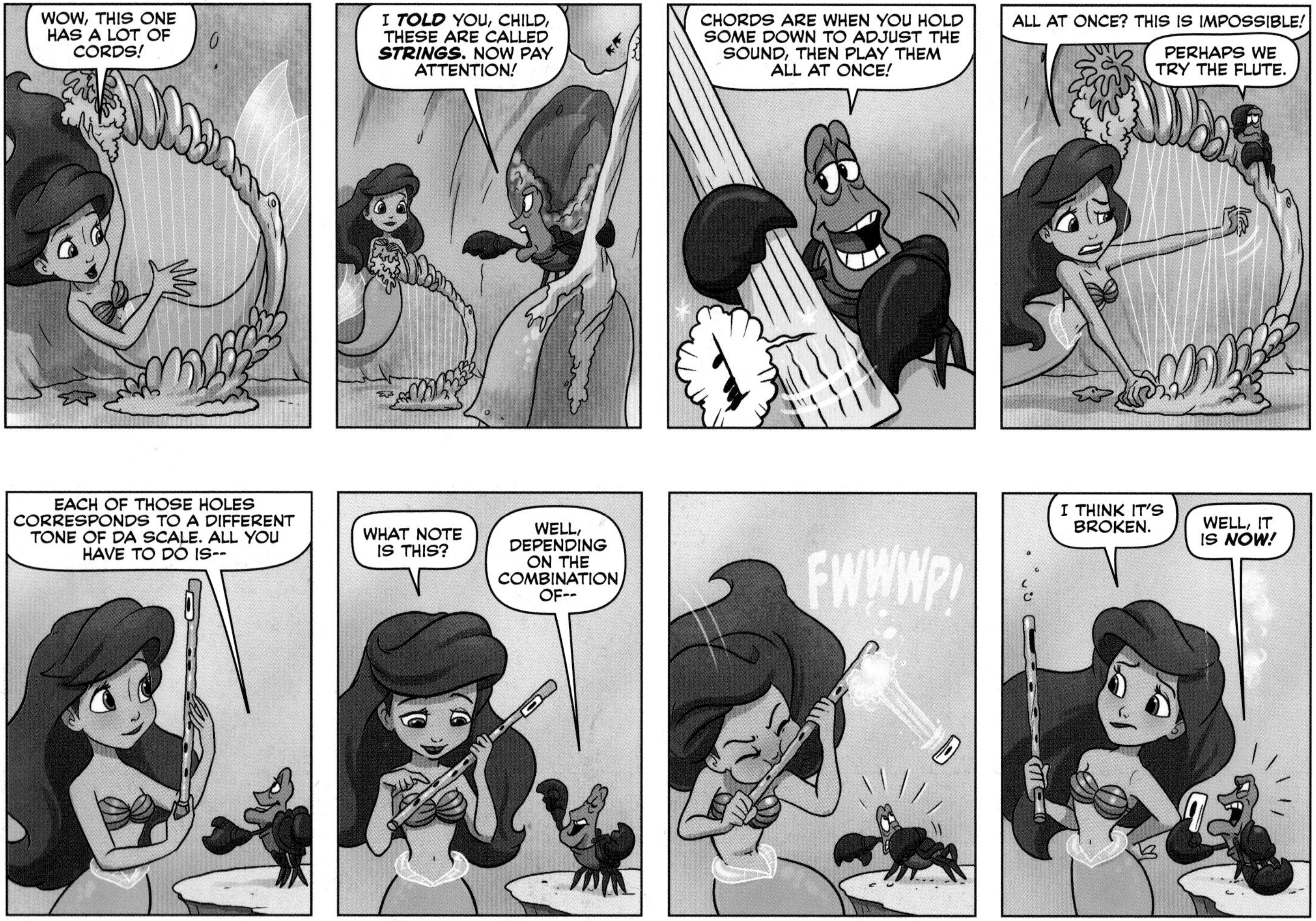
WOW, THIS ONE HAS A LOT OF CORDS!
I TOLD YOU, CHILD, THESE ARE CALLED STRINGS. NOW PAY ATTENTION!
CHORDS ARE WHEN YOU HOLD SOME DOWN TO ADJUST THE SOUND, THEN PLAY THEM ALL AT ONCE!
ALL AT ONCE? THIS IS IMPOSSIBLE!
PERHAPS WE TRY THE FLUTE.
EACH OF THOSE HOLES CORRESPONDS TO A DIFFERENT TONE OF DA SCALE. ALL YOU HAVE TO DO IS--
WHAT NOTE IS THIS?
WELL, DEPENDING ON THE COMBINATION OF--
FWWWP!
I THINK IT'S BROKEN.
WELL, IT IS NOW!

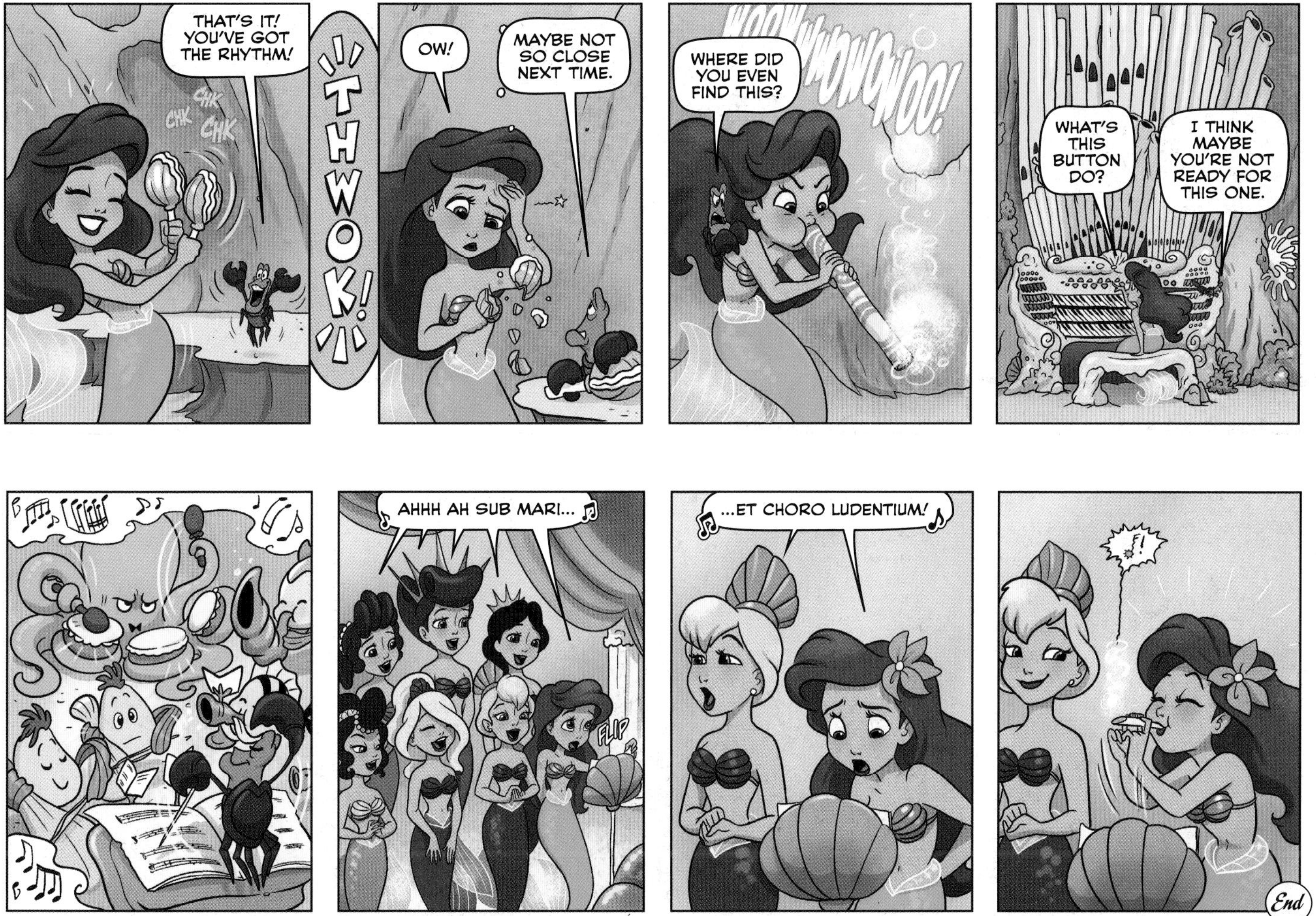

THAT'S IT! YOU'VE GOT THE RHYTHM!
CHK CHK CHK
THWOK!
OW!
MAYBE NOT SO CLOSE NEXT TIME.
WHERE DID YOU EVEN FIND THIS?
WOOWWWOWOWOO!
WHAT'S THIS BUTTON DO?
I THINK MAYBE YOU'RE NOT READY FOR THIS ONE.
AHHH AH SUB MARI...
FLIP
...ET CHORO LUDENTIUM!
F!
End

BIBBIDI BOBBIDI FLU

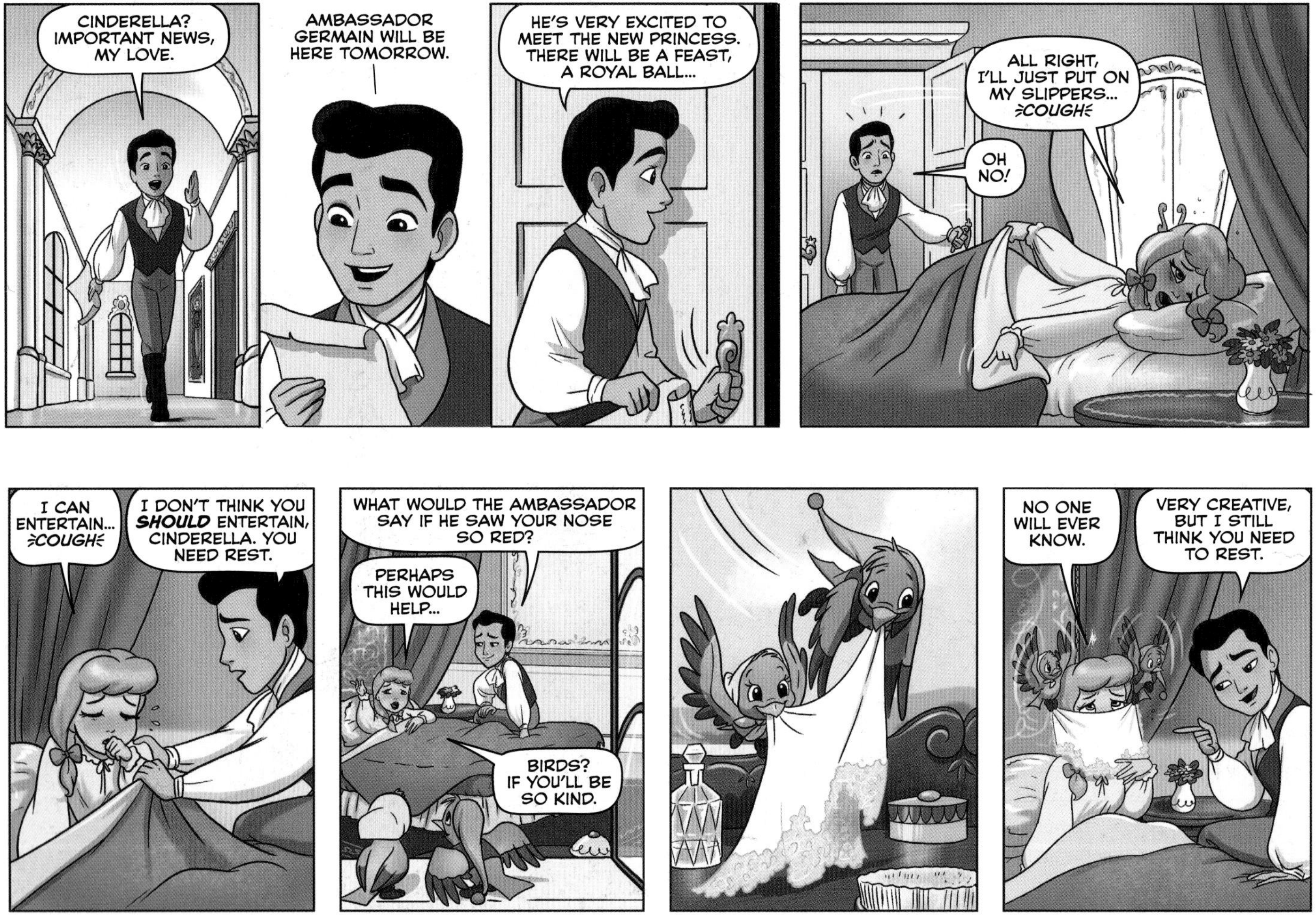

CINDERELLA? IMPORTANT NEWS, MY LOVE.
AMBASSADOR GERMAIN WILL BE HERE TOMORROW.
HE'S VERY EXCITED TO MEET THE NEW PRINCESS. THERE WILL BE A FEAST, A ROYAL BALL...
ALL RIGHT, I'LL JUST PUT ON MY SLIPPERS... COUGH
OH NO!
I CAN ENTERTAIN... COUGH
I DON'T THINK YOU SHOULD ENTERTAIN, CINDERELLA. YOU NEED REST.
WHAT WOULD THE AMBASSADOR SAY IF HE SAW YOUR NOSE SO RED?
PERHAPS THIS WOULD HELP...
BIRDS? IF YOU'LL BE SO KIND.
NO ONE WILL EVER KNOW.
VERY CREATIVE, BUT I STILL THINK YOU NEED TO REST.

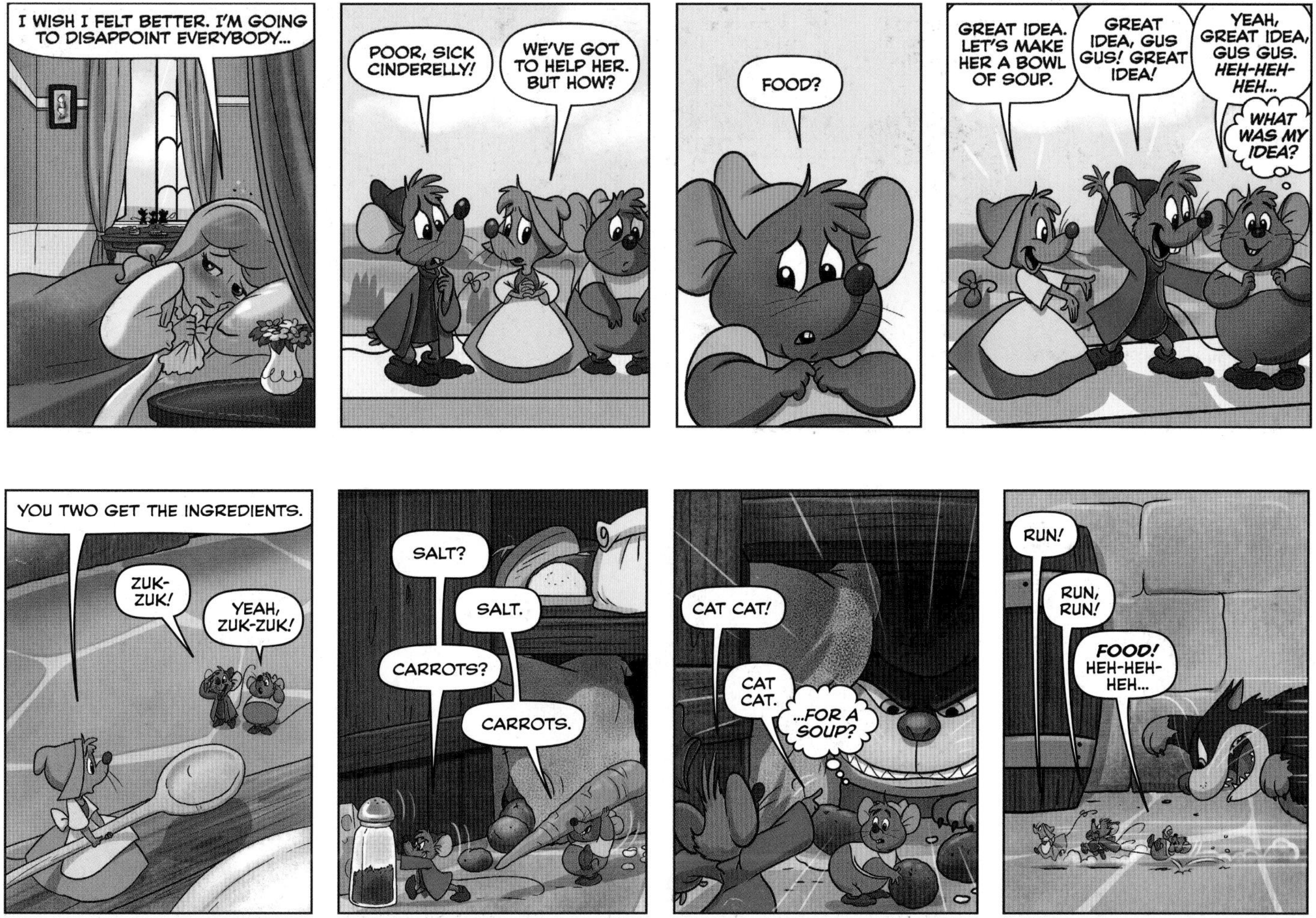
I WISH I FELT BETTER. I'M GOING TO DISAPPOINT EVERYBODY...
POOR, SICK CINDERELLY!
WE'VE GOT TO HELP HER. BUT HOW?
FOOD?
GREAT IDEA. LET'S MAKE HER A BOWL OF SOUP.
GREAT IDEA, GUS GUS! GREAT IDEA!
YEAH, GREAT IDEA, GUS GUS. *HEH-HEH-HEH...*
WHAT WAS MY IDEA?
YOU TWO GET THE INGREDIENTS.
ZUK-ZUK!
YEAH, ZUK-ZUK!
SALT?
SALT.
CARROTS?
CARROTS.
CAT CAT!
CAT CAT.
...FOR A SOUP?
RUN!
RUN, RUN!
FOOD! HEH-HEH-HEH...

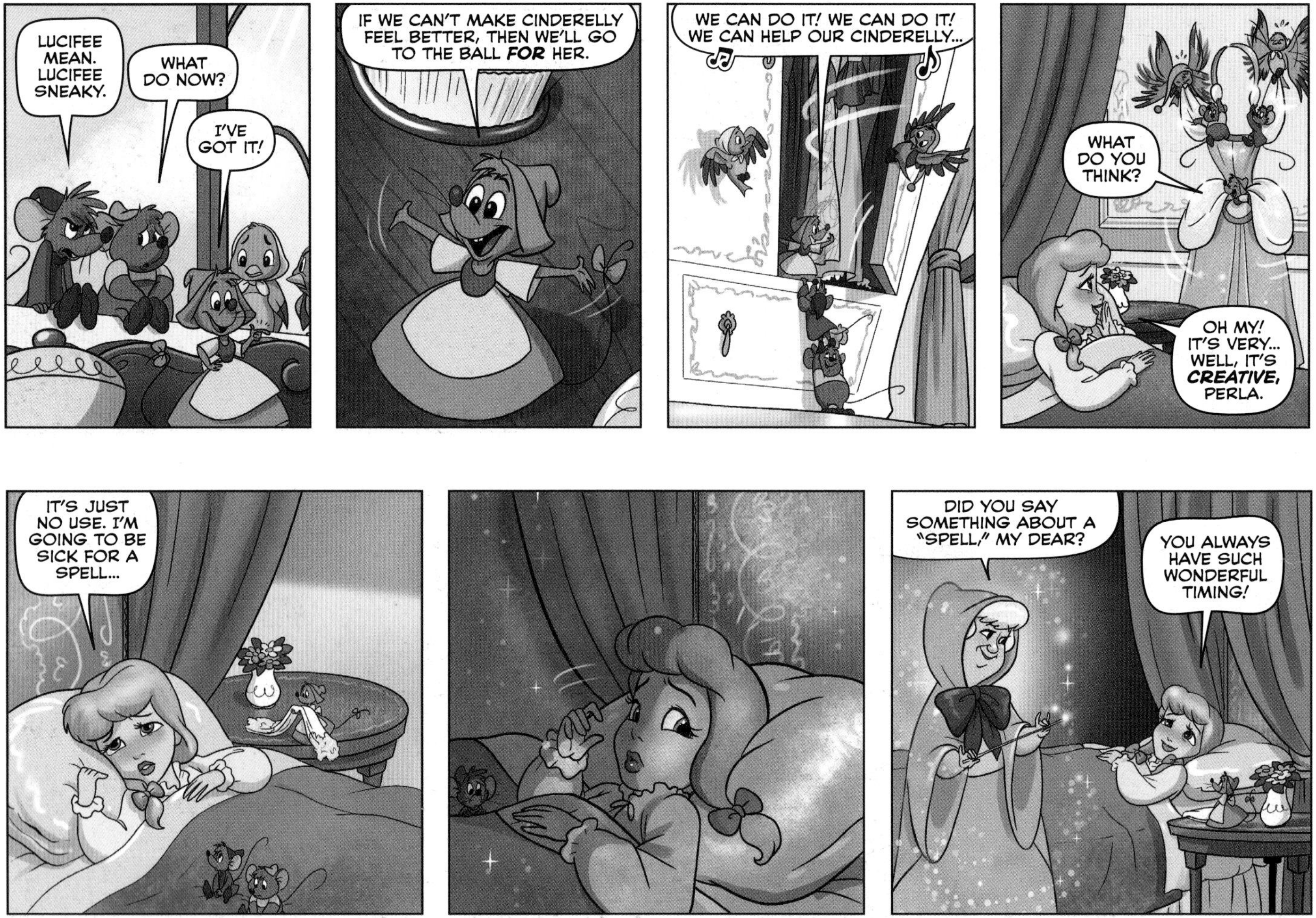
LUCIFEE MEAN. LUCIFEE SNEAKY.
WHAT DO NOW?
I'VE GOT IT!
IF WE CAN'T MAKE CINDERELLY FEEL BETTER, THEN WE'LL GO TO THE BALL **FOR** HER.
WE CAN DO IT! WE CAN DO IT! WE CAN HELP OUR CINDERELLY...
WHAT DO YOU THINK?
OH MY! IT'S VERY... WELL, IT'S ***CREATIVE***, PERLA.
IT'S JUST NO USE. I'M GOING TO BE SICK FOR A SPELL...
DID YOU SAY SOMETHING ABOUT A "SPELL," MY DEAR?
YOU ALWAYS HAVE SUCH WONDERFUL TIMING!

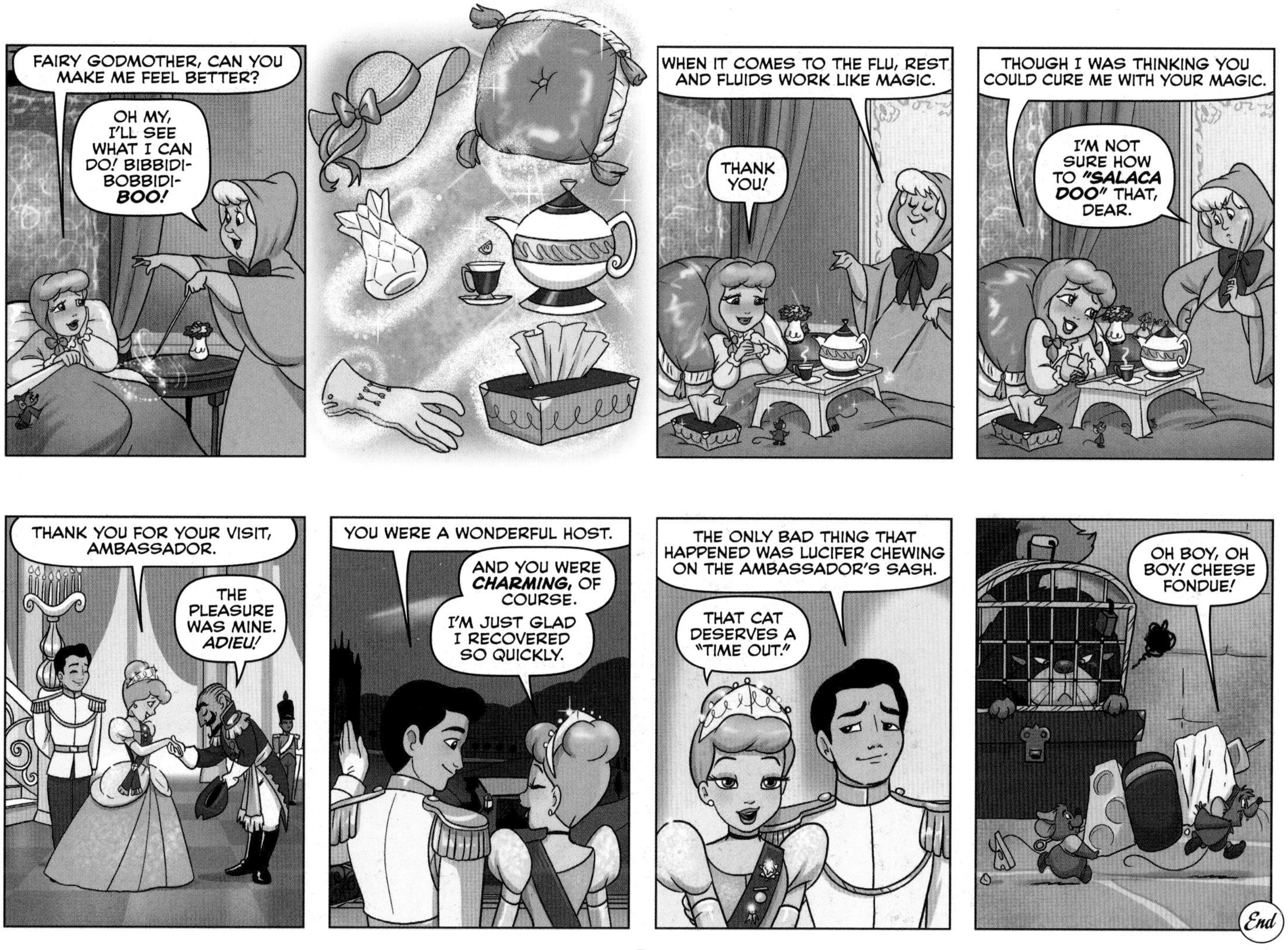
FAIRY GODMOTHER, CAN YOU MAKE ME FEEL BETTER?
OH MY, I'LL SEE WHAT I CAN DO! BIBBIDI-BOBBIDI-BOO!
WHEN IT COMES TO THE FLU, REST AND FLUIDS WORK LIKE MAGIC.
THANK YOU!
THOUGH I WAS THINKING YOU COULD CURE ME WITH YOUR MAGIC.
I'M NOT SURE HOW TO "SALACA DOO" THAT, DEAR.
THANK YOU FOR YOUR VISIT, AMBASSADOR.
THE PLEASURE WAS MINE. ADIEU!
YOU WERE A WONDERFUL HOST.
AND YOU WERE CHARMING, OF COURSE.
I'M JUST GLAD I RECOVERED SO QUICKLY.
THE ONLY BAD THING THAT HAPPENED WAS LUCIFER CHEWING ON THE AMBASSADOR'S SASH.
THAT CAT DESERVES A "TIME OUT."
OH BOY, OH BOY! CHEESE FONDUE!
End

EMBROIDERY

THERE'S NOTHING MORE *BORING* THAN EMBROIDERY.

A LADY FINDS A WAY TO MAKE *ANY* TASK INTERESTING.

End

MOOD WIND

WSHHHSSSHHH

WWWWWWHHSSSSHHHH

THE WIND DOESN'T FEEL LIKE TALKING TODAY.

End

KITCHEN HAND

I'VE GOT A PRINCE IN MY DINING ROOM AND AN ALLIGATOR IN MY BAND—

—BUT I WILL *NOT* LET A FLY LIVE IN MY *GUMBO!*

COME ON LADY, IT'S *COLD* OUTSIDE!

NO FLIES IN THE KITCHEN. *OUT!*

AREN'T YOU THE ONE AND ONLY TIANA, ONCE TURNED INTO A FROG AND FRIENDS WITH INSECT AND ANIMAL ALIKE?

I WAS A FROG FOR A WHILE AND I WAS FRIENDS WITH A FIREFLY.

THAT'S WHAT I THOUGHT.

BUT YOU'RE SWIMMING IN MY *GUMBO!*

ISN'T THAT WHAT FRIENDS ARE *FOR?*

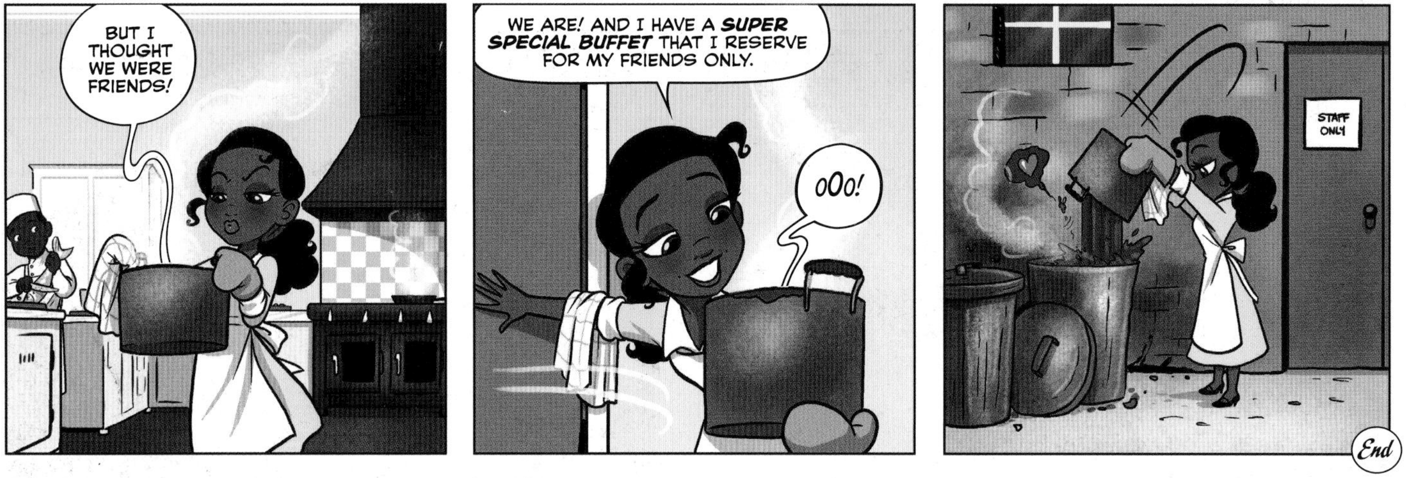
BUT I THOUGHT WE WERE FRIENDS!
WE ARE! AND I HAVE A **SUPER SPECIAL BUFFET** THAT I RESERVE FOR MY FRIENDS ONLY.
oOo!
STAFF ONLY
End

NEW FRIENDS

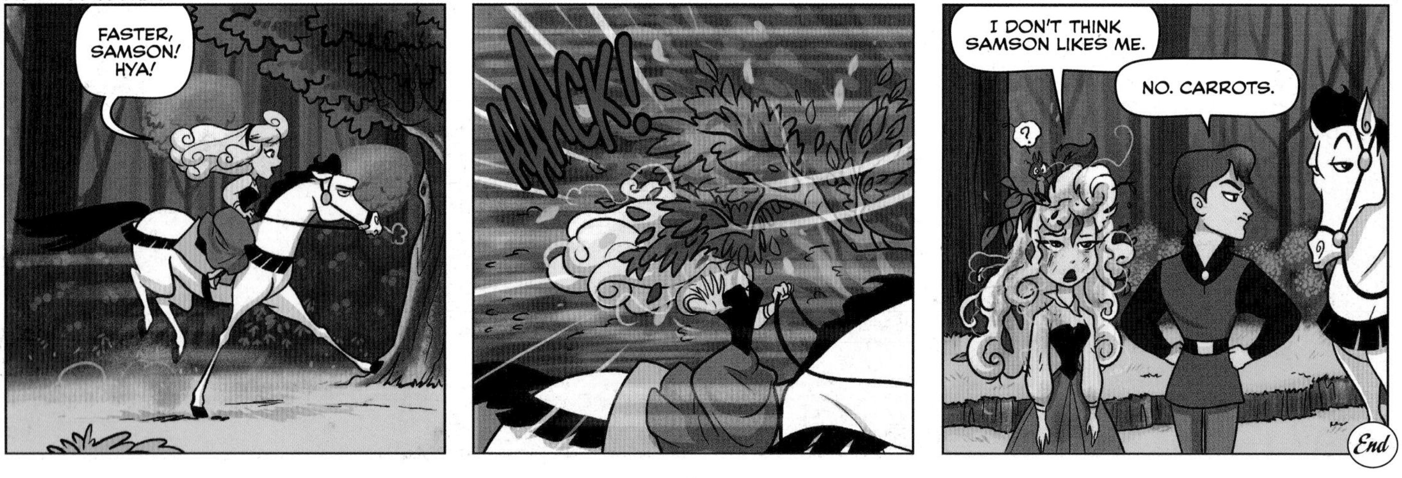
FASTER, SAMSON! HYA!
AAACK!
I DON'T THINK SAMSON LIKES ME.
?
NO. CARROTS.
End

IS IT ME, OR HAS JASMINE BEEN REALLY *QUIET* LATELY?

YOU SHOULD KNOW WHAT IT'S LIKE BEING COOPED UP BY YOURSELF.

Y'MEAN SHE'S... *LONELY?*

UNTIL ALADDIN GETS BACK FROM HIS TRIP, I GUESS SO...

POOR KID.

HOP ON, GIRLFRIEND, *WE'RE GOING SHOPPING!*

SALÂM, YOUR HIGHNESS! JUST BROWSING TODAY?

MAYBE. DO YOU HAVE ANYTHING NEW?

AAH, YES! BEHOLD THIS *EXQUISITE* ENSEMBLE FROM OUR NEWLY-ARRIVED *WINTER* COLLECTION!

HOLD THIS; I NEED A CHANGING ROOM.

I'LL TAKE *TEN!*

THANKS FOR THE SHOPPING DAY, GENIE!

ANYTIME, JAS!

≥PHEW≤ I THINK WE SHOPPED A LITTLE **TOO HARD.**

SHAME ON YOU; THERE'S NO SUCH THING!

BESIDES, WE HAVE OL' **EL RUGGO** TO CARRY IT ALL HOME.

FINE, I'LL LEAVE THE SHOES.

End

DUCKLINGS

WHAT DID YOU **DO** TO IT?!

IF YOU WANTED **DUCKLINGS** ON IT, YOU SHOULD HAVE SAID.

End

I HAVE A SPECIAL INVITATION FOR YOU ALL.

OH BOY!

I WANT YOU TO BE MY GUESTS AT THE ROYAL BALL AND DANCE WITH ME.

HOORAY!

YOU KNOW HOW TO *WALTZ*, DON'T YOU?

OH NO!

NO NEED TO WORRY. I'LL TEACH YOU.

SEE WHAT I MEAN? THERE'S ALWAYS A CATCH WITH HER!

NOW, UH, LISTEN HERE, MEN. WE HAVE NOTHING TO BE NERVOUS ABOUT. IT'S JUST *DANCY FANCIN'* WITH OUR QUEEN. ER, *FANCY DANCIN'* IS WHAT I MEAN.

THAT'S RIGHT, DOC. I'LL SHOW YOU THE STEPS.

SOUNDS GOOD. LET ME JUST TIGHTEN UP MY TROUSERS.

GET MY SPECTACLES SPIC 'N' SPAN.

30 MINUTES LATER.

JUST NEED TO RECALIBRATE MY CAP...

WOULD ANYONE *ELSE* LIKE TO GO FIRST?

THAT'S VERY GOOD, SNEEZY. NOW LET'S TRY A SPIN.

ALRIGHT. I'LL DO WHAT I CAN!

AHHHH... AHHHH...

AHHHH-CHOOOOOO!

NO, SNEEZY! YOU'RE SUPPOSED TO SPIN *ME* AROUND.

NOW SHE TELLS ME.

ARE YOU SURE YOU'RE AWAKE ENOUGH TO DANCE, SLEEPY?

READY AND ABLE.

MAYBE YOU SHOULD TAKE A LITTLE NAP.

I'LL BE... FINE.

I'VE GOT AN IDEA. WAIT RIGHT THERE.

OH DEAR! I DON'T THINK WE CAN BRING YOUR BED TO THE ROYAL BALL.

...THEN WE SHOULD...USE A BED...FROM THE PALACE... ZZZ...

SLEEP

I DO LOVE HOW YOU'RE ALWAYS SO HAPPY, HAPPY.

I LOVE IT, TOO, MA'AM! *HA HA HA!*

BUT A ROYAL BALL IS VERY *SOPHISTICATED.* WILL YOU BE ABLE TO ACT SOPHISTICATED?

WHY, I AIN'T EVEN ABLE TO PRONOUNCE...THAT WORD. *HA HA HA!*

BUT I'LL TRY, MA'AM. HERE I GO.

I THINK HE'S GONNA EXPLODE!

OH MY.

SOPHISTIMACATED HOGWASH!

BASHFUL, WOULD YOU LIKE TO DANCE WITH ME?

OHHHHHHHHHH GOSH! I WOULD LOVE TO.

WONDERFUL!

NOW, WOULD YOU LIKE TO STOP HIDING UNDERNEATH THAT BENCH?

OHHHHHHHHHH GOSH! I DON'T THINK SO.

OW! DOPEY, WATCH YOUR--OW!

PAY ATTENTION TO--OW!

OWWW! OH, THAT HURTS!

DOPEY, SHE TOLD US **NOT** TO STEP ON HER FEET! **DON'T** STEP ON HER FEET!

THAT'S OKAY, DOPEY. WE CAN KEEP DANCING, I'LL JUST CHANGE INTO THESE **WOODEN** SHOES.

WHEN'RE YA GONNA FACE FACTS? YOU'LL NEVER LEARN US HOW TO DANCE AT A ROYAL BALL.

OH, GRUMPY. DON'T SAY THAT.

ALL WE KNOWS IS THAT SILLY DANCIN', AND THAT AIN'T FIT FOR RACCOONS, LET ALONE ROYALTY.

I MEAN, ONLY A KING 'ER **QUEEN** COULD MAKE SILLY DANCIN' OKAY AT A ROYAL BALL!

WHY, OF COURSE. I'M A QUEEN!

GRUMPY, I COULD KISS YOU!

NOT IF YA CAN'T CATCH ME!

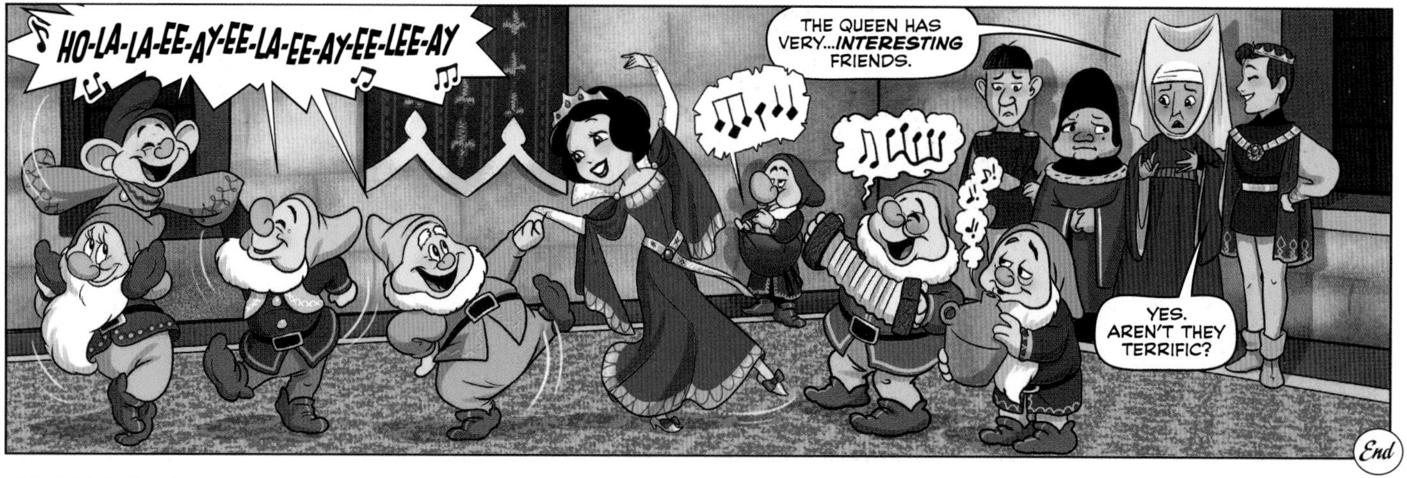
HO-LA-LA-EE-AY-EE-LA-EE-AY-EE-LEE-AY
THE QUEEN HAS VERY...**INTERESTING** FRIENDS.
YES. AREN'T THEY TERRIFIC?
End

TUMBLEWEEDS

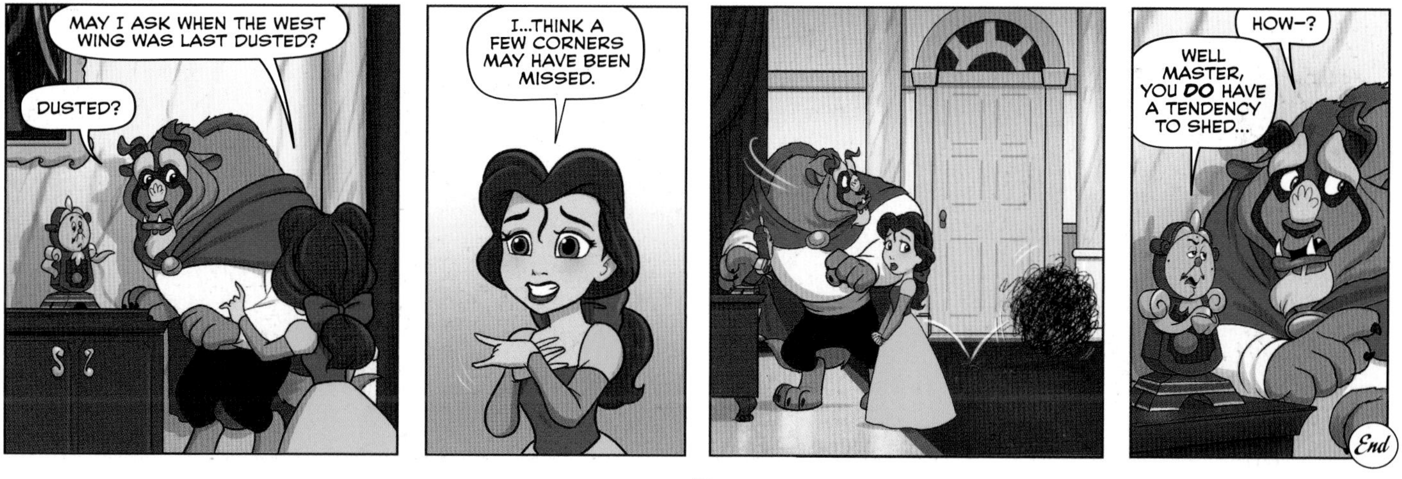
MAY I ASK WHEN THE WEST WING WAS LAST DUSTED?
DUSTED?
I...THINK A FEW CORNERS MAY HAVE BEEN MISSED.
HOW–?
WELL MASTER, YOU **DO** HAVE A TENDENCY TO SHED...
End

BAKING DAY

OOOH, THE MUFFINS ARE DONE.

AWW, I DIDN'T THINK THIS RECIPE WOULD MAKE SO *MANY!*

MOTHER AND I CAN'T POSSIBLY EAT THEM *ALL* BY *OURSELVES.*

SUCH A WASTE.

End

WHAT ARE FRIENDS FOR?

FLOUNDER, LOOK! A NEW SHIPWRECK WE HAVEN'T EX--

:WULP:

SEBASTIAAAAANN...

ALL DAT ACADEMY TRAINING...

End

WHATCHA WEARIN' TO MARDIS GRAS, TIA HONEY?

ACTUALLY, I'M NOT GOING. WE'RE HOSTING A WEDDING AT THE PALACE--

BRUNCH AT DUKE'S CAFE...

AWWWW! THAT'S TOO, TOO BAD. BUT GUESS WHAT? AH'M GONNA BE DRESSED AS A *FAIRY PRINCESS!* CAN YA BELIEVE IT?

OH, I BELIEVE IT.

MY DRESS IS GONNA SHIMMER LIKE A SHOOTIN' STAR, WITH DIAMOND ENCRUSTED WINGS, AND I GOT EARRIN'S THAT LOOK LIKE TINY, *BABY,* FAIRIES. *AIEEE,* SO CUTE!

IT'S GONNA LOOK LIKE AH'M FLYIN' THROUGH THE CLOUDS ON FAIRY DUST!

CHARLOTTE, WATCHING YOU IS MORE ENTERTAINING THAN *TEN* MARDIS GRAS.

...AND EACH WING OF MY DRESS'LL HAVE TINY JEWELS SEWN IN!

OOH, PRETTY...

THIS NEEDS SOMETHING...

A LITTLE HOT SAUCE WILL MAKE IT THE BEE'S KNEES!

NOPE, I CAN STILL FEEL MY TONGUE. GONNA NEED A WHOLE LOT MORE.

...AND THERE ARE LIL' MIRRORS IN THE WINGS, SO I CAN CHECK MY MAKE-UP *ON THE FLOAT.* THAT WAS *MAH* IDEA...

...THEN THERE'S THE QUESTION OF MY SHOES, BECAUSE AH'VE GOT **SO** MANY CHOICES...

I THINK THERE'S SOME **EXTRA SPICY** SAUCE IN MY PURSE.

REDHO JAZZ HOT SAUCE It'll have ya Whistling Dixie!

⸓WHOO⸓

TOO MILD. I MUST'VE LEFT IT IN MY PURSE TOO LONG.

...'CAUSE THEY SAID THEY'D SEW WINGS ONTO THE SHOES, BUT AH WORRY THOSE WINGS'LL DISTRACT FROM MY OTHER WINGS...

A-HA! I KNEW THE GOOD STUFF WAS AROUND HERE SOMEWHERE.

THAT SAUCE IS **WICKED**, TIANA. WATCH YO'SELF!

TIANA SITS BACK DOWN FOR BRUNCH.

...AH WAS JUST **APPALLED** BY HOW LITTLE FAIRY JEWELRY THEY HAD...

ALL RIGHT, THIS SAUCE HAS GOTTA BE HOT ENOUGH.

REALLY? THIS ONE IS WEAKER'N A BABY KITTEN!

...AH WAS SO UPSET AT HIM, AH WAS PRACTICALLY FUMIN'...

OH, THIS KITTEN'S GOT CLAWS! THIS KITTEN'S GOT CLAWS!

...SO AH'M PRACTICING MAH WAVE FOR THE FLOAT, CAUSE YA GOTTA HAVE JUST THE RIGHT WAVE...

TOO HOT! TOO HOT!

...AND THIS HANDSOME MAN SEES ME WAVING ON THE BENCH IN THE PARK...

...AND SO AH SAY, "IF ONLY SOME TALL DRINK OF WATER COULD HELP ME DOWN FROM HERE"...

THIS IS **NOT** WORKING...

SPLOOSH

MY MOUTH IS **BURNING!**

HERE'S A SODA POP, MISS!

OH **NO**, SODA WILL MAKE IT WORSE!

LEMME TRY FANNING YOUR TONGUE.

DUKES MENU

'OWWW, I'S S'ILL BUR'ING!

THERE'S ONLY ONE WAY TO CURE THIS!

MORE HOT SAUCE! WE GOTTA COUNTERACT THE FIRST ONE!

HELP!

DOES ANYBODY HERE KNOW A CURE FOR HOT SAUCE BURNIN'?

FLOUR

I WILL NEVER TASTE ANYTHING AGAIN!

THIS IS RIDICULOUS, I NEED SOMETHING ELSE...

THERE!

MILK

glug glug glug

AAAAAHHH!

MILK

HOT SAUCE IS... THE BEE'S KNEES... AND MILK IS... *THE BUG SPRAY.*

MILK

...AND THAT'S HOW AH DECIDED TO FORGET THE GLOVES AND JUST MAKE MAH *FINGERNAILS* SPARKLE.

WHAT DO YA THINK, TIA? DOES MAH OUTFIT SOUND WONDERFUL?

YEAH, CHARLOTTE. I THINK IT'LL BE *RED HOT*.

OH GOODIE, GOODIE, *GOODIE!*

End

BUCKETHEAD TWO

GOOD MORNING, MY PRINCE BUCKETHEAD. DID YOU SLEEP WELL?

OH, I'M *SO* GLAD!

I REALLY CAN'T STOP; I HAVE TO FINISH MOPPING THE SCULLERY.

WELL...I GUESS I *COULD* STAY A MINUTE.

IF YOU INSIST.

HE'S A LITTLE SHY.

End

MATCHMAKER

SO... YOU WANT TO MEET NEW PEOPLE, BUT YOU'RE... AFRAID?

AYE.

MAYBE IF WE START WITH YOUR APPEARANCE, PROUD MACGUFFIN STOCK...

SAY, A NICE LASSIE SAYS HELLO. WHAT COULD YOU WEAR TO MAKE YOU FEEL CONFIDENT?

OKAY, MIGHT BE OVERDOING IT A WEE STRETCH.

End

LATE NIGHT READS

MADEMOISELLE, MAY I ASK HOW MUCH LONGER??

JUST SIX MORE CHAPTERS, YOU'LL BE FINE!

FRESH CUP OF TEA?

OH, I'M NOT TIRED AT ALL, MRS POTTS, YOU DIDN'T HAVE TO...

I WAS TALKING TO LUMIERE, DEAR..

ZZZ...

End

IT'S SUCH A LOVELY DAY, AND I HAVEN'T BEEN ON A WALK IN THE WOODS IN SO LONG.

NEITHER HAVE I! THAT'S A FANTASTIC IDEA!

LET ME JUST GET READY!

READY!

HOW FAR DID YOU PLAN ON WALKING?

LOOK AT THIS! WE DIDN'T EVEN NEED TO PACK A LUNCH.

WAIT! DON'T EAT THAT!

?

AURORA, I'VE BEEN OUT AND ABOUT MYSELF, AND I KNOW THESE APPLES ARE PERFECTLY SAFE.

I'M SURE THE WORM FELT THE SAME WAY.

BLORCH!

LISTEN! THAT'S A WHITE WAGTAIL. OVER THERE!

THEY'RE QUITE SHY.

BE GENTLE!

DON'T WORRY! IT SENSES I'M NOT A THREAT. PERHAPS MY GENTLE DEMEANOR.

OR THE COMPANY YOU KEEP?

THIS SPOT LOOKS NICE!

WHY DON'T WE MOVE A LITTLE MORE DOWN THE HILL.

BUT THE SHADE IS PERFECT HERE AND THERE'S NOTHING AROUND TO DISTURB US!

LIKE WE JUST DISTURBED THAT ANT COLONY?

BE CAREFUL. THOSE ROCKS CAN BE--

SPLASH

SLIPPERY.

I'M NOT USUALLY SO CLUMSY. I'M JUST NERVOUS, I SUPPOSE.

I KNOW. WE DANCE *BEAUTIFULLY*, MY DARLING.

WHILE YOU'RE IN THERE, THOUGH...

I FEEL SO STUPID. YOU WERE RAISED IN THESE WOODS, AFTER ALL...

BELIEVE IT OR NOT, UNLIKE EVERYONE ELSE IN THE CASTLE, I DID SPEND TIME IN THE FOREST.

IT'S ALL RIGHT, I'M JUST HAPPY TO HAVE SOMEONE TO SHARE ALL THIS WITH!

NEXT TIME WE JUST WON'T BRING HOME AS MANY NEW FRIENDS.

End

33

CARPET SALE

WISE COUNCIL

THE DREAM ROUTINE

QUE QUE NA-TO-RA..

...YOU WILL UNDERSTAND...

GOOD DAY, CHILD.

GRANDMOTHER WILLOW, I CAME TO TELL YOU ABOUT A DREAM I HAD LAST NIGHT.

OOOH, A *DREAM!* I DO LIKE A GOOD DREAM!

I KNOW YOU DO.

WAIT, IS THIS THE ONE WHERE PEOPLE GROW LEAVES ON THEIR ARMS?

NO...

OH, PITY. I LIKE THAT ONE.

IN MY DREAM, I WAS SITTING ON A HILL...

I LOOKED UP AT THE SKY AND SAW TWO CLOUDS.

ONE CLOUD WAS SHAPED LIKE A HILL. THE OTHER WAS SHAPED LIKE ME, SITTING.

AND THAT'S NOT EVEN THE MOST INTERESTING PART!

MY FRONDS TREMBLE IN ANTICIPATION, DEAR...

MEEKO WAS IN MY DREAM!

WE JUST... *STARED* AT ONE ANOTHER FOR A MINUTE OR SO.

AND THEN, HE DECIDED TO LEAVE. SO...HE LEFT!

?!

AND THAT'S NOT EVEN THE MOST INTERESTING PART!

I AM *GREATLY* ANTICIPATING THE "INTERESTING PART," DEAR.

IN THIS DREAM, I WAS APPROACHED BY A MIGHTY STAG!

AH, *NOW* IT'S GETTING INTERESTING...

IT BECKONED ME TO SPEAK WITH HIM.

FASCINATING!

UNDER GLINTS OF MOONLIGHT, THE STAG STOOD PROUD AND TOLD ME THESE WORDS...

WHAT DID HE SAY, CHILD? WHAT DID HE SAY?

HE ASKED ME FOR TURN-BY-TURN DIRECTIONS TO THE NEAREST RIVER! SO I DREW HIM A LITTLE MAP...

I THINK THIS *DREAM* IS GOING TO PUT ME TO *SLEEP*.

THEN, IN MY DREAM, I TURNED INTO A PINECONE.

WELL, IT WAS A PINECONE, BUT IT WAS ALSO A LEAF.

I HAD THE THIN STEM OF A LEAF, BUT THE SCALES OF A PINECONE.

DOES THAT MAKE SENSE?

IT MAKES ME WONDER WHAT YOU ATE FOR DINNER LAST NIGHT, CHILD...

WHAT *DO* YOU THINK MY DREAM MEANT, GRANDMOTHER WILLOW?

THE DREAM MEANT...UH, *EAT WELL, SLEEP WELL, AND BE WELL!*

BUT GRANDMOTHER, YOU SAID THAT ABOUT THE *LAST* DREAM I TOLD YOU!

IT WORKED, DIDN'T IT?

MAYBE I'LL ASK KEKATA NEXT TIME...

DO **YOU** THINK THAT'S WHAT MY DREAM MEANT, MEEKO? "EAT WELL, SLEEP WELL, AND BE WELL?"

Z

AS ALWAYS, GRANDMOTHER WILLOW IS RIGHT.

Z

End

THE SMOULDER

OH COME ON, PLEASE?!

NO, YOU CAN'T PLAY WITH PASCAL, HE JUST ATE AND NEEDS A NAP!

Z

MMM?

THAT HAS **NEVER** WORKED ON ME.

NEITHER HAS "LOST PUPPY."

End

THIS PLACE GIVES ME THE CREEPS...

QUIT BEING SUCH A *GUPPY*, FLOUNDER!

YOU'LL NEVER FIND ANYTHING COOL IN SUCH A DARK, SCARY PLACE.

OH NO?

UNBELIEVABLE!

I'VE NEVER SEEN ANYTHING THIS COOL BEFORE IN MY ENTIRE LIFE!

ISN'T IT INCREDIBLE?

SCUTTLE, YOU'LL NEVER BELIEVE WHAT WE FOUND TODAY!

THAT MAKES TWO OF US, SWEETIE.

DO YOU KNOW WHAT THIS IS?

OH, WHAT? *THIS?* OF COURSE I KNOW WHAT THIS IS!

AFTER ALL, I AM A *CERTIFICATIONAL* AUTHORITY ON HUMAN STUFF.

IT'S REMARKABLE HOW THEY MANAGE TO GET *ANOTHER BIRD* INTO HERE.

CALLED... A *FLIBBERBOBBIN.*

LET'S SAY A HUMAN GETS THEIR CLOTHES WET.

THEY HATE THAT.

THEY JUST HANG THEIR WET WEARABLES OFF THIS OL' FLIBBERBOBBIN. IN A FEW HOURS, THEIR CLOTHES GO FROM SOAKING WET TO A LITTLE MOIST. JUST THE WAY HUMANS LIKE!

SO COOL....

DAT IS DE CRAZIEST MUMBO JUMBO I HAVE EVER HEARD.

WOW...

SEBASTIAN, WHAT ARE YOU DOING HERE?

YOU ARE LATE TO REHEARSAL FOR DE SPRING CONCERT. *AGAIN.* THE PIKE WHO PLAYS FIFE SPOTTED YOU WERE HERE.

AND IF YOU PAID ATTENTION IN MUSIC CLASS, YOU WOULD KNOW DIS HAS GOT TO BE A MUSICAL INSTRUMENT. LISTEN,

CLEARLY, IT IS BROKEN.

YOU'RE CRAZY! HOW ARE YOU SUPPOSED TO MAKE MUSIC WITH A *CLOTHES DRYER?*

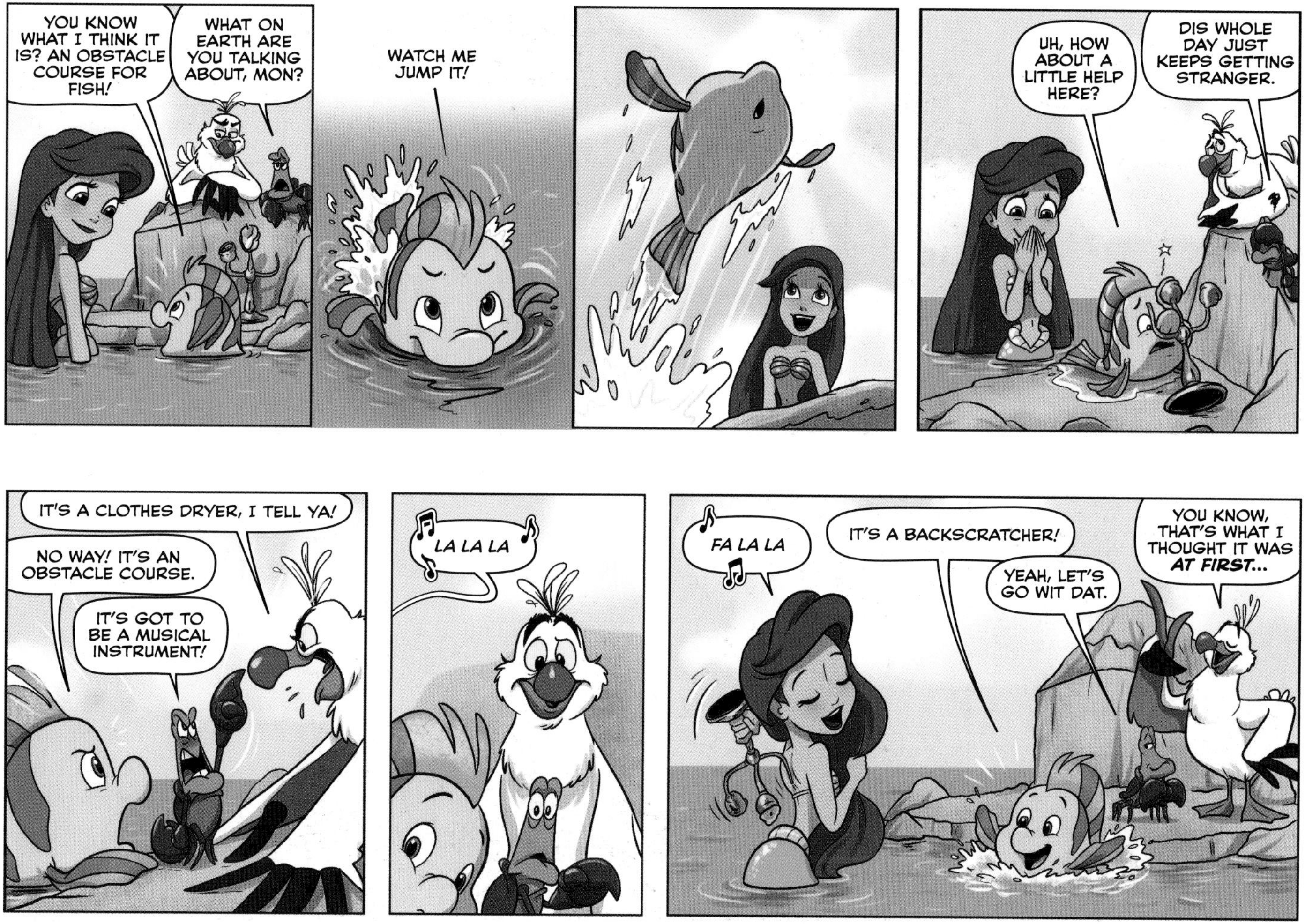
YOU KNOW WHAT I THINK IT IS? AN OBSTACLE COURSE FOR FISH!
WHAT ON EARTH ARE YOU TALKING ABOUT, MON?
WATCH ME JUMP IT!
UH, HOW ABOUT A LITTLE HELP HERE?
DIS WHOLE DAY JUST KEEPS GETTING STRANGER.
IT'S A CLOTHES DRYER, I TELL YA!
NO WAY! IT'S AN OBSTACLE COURSE.
IT'S GOT TO BE A MUSICAL INSTRUMENT!
LA LA LA
FA LA LA
IT'S A BACKSCRATCHER!
YEAH, LET'S GO WIT DAT.
YOU KNOW, THAT'S WHAT I THOUGHT IT WAS ***AT FIRST...***

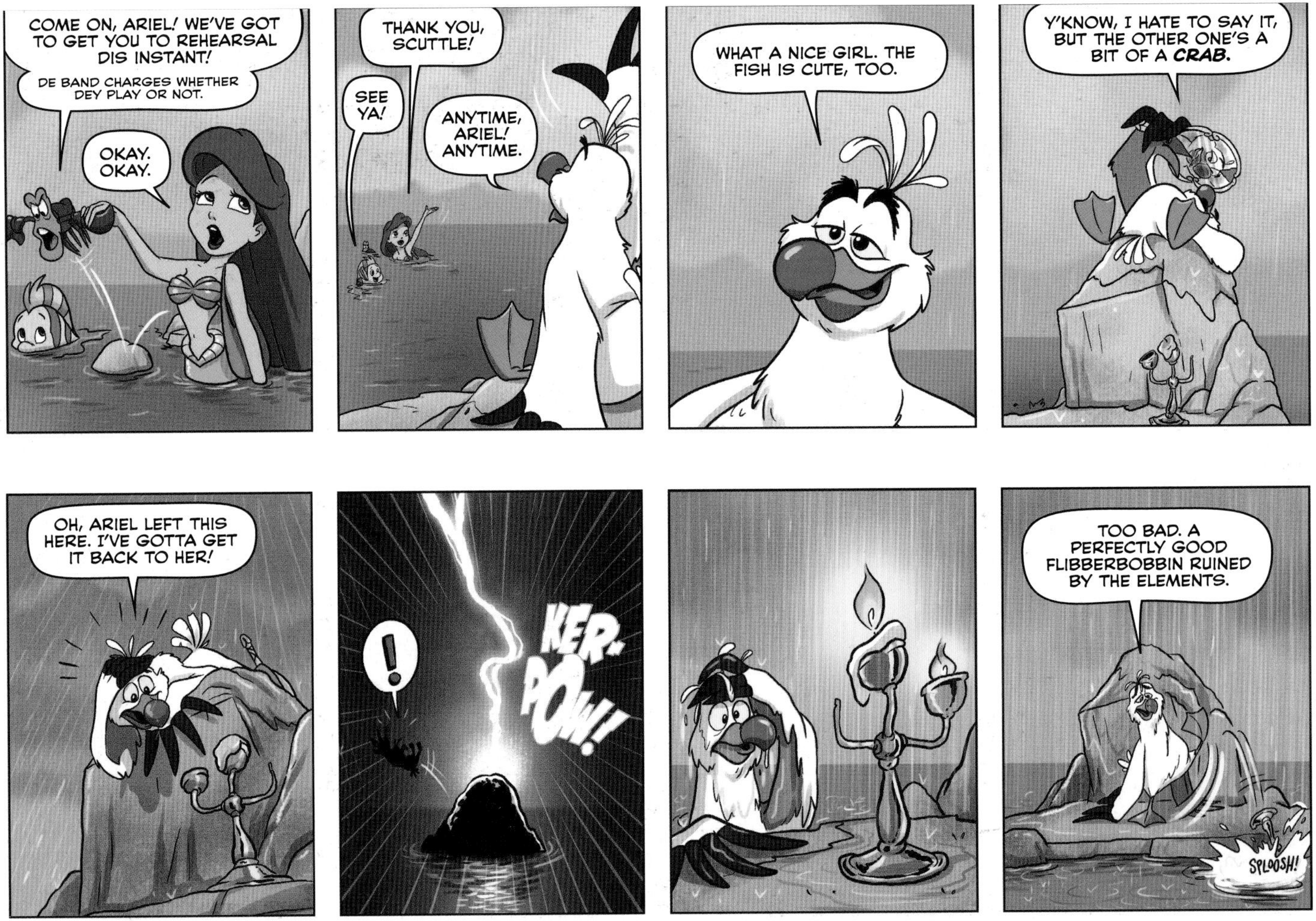
COME ON, ARIEL! WE'VE GOT TO GET YOU TO REHEARSAL DIS INSTANT!
DE BAND CHARGES WHETHER DEY PLAY OR NOT.
OKAY. OKAY.
THANK YOU, SCUTTLE!
SEE YA!
ANYTIME, ARIEL! ANYTIME.
WHAT A NICE GIRL. THE FISH IS CUTE, TOO.
Y'KNOW, I HATE TO SAY IT, BUT THE OTHER ONE'S A BIT OF A **CRAB.**
OH, ARIEL LEFT THIS HERE. I'VE GOTTA GET IT BACK TO HER!
!
KER-POW!!
TOO BAD. A PERFECTLY GOOD FLIBBERBOBBIN RUINED BY THE ELEMENTS.
SPLOOSH!

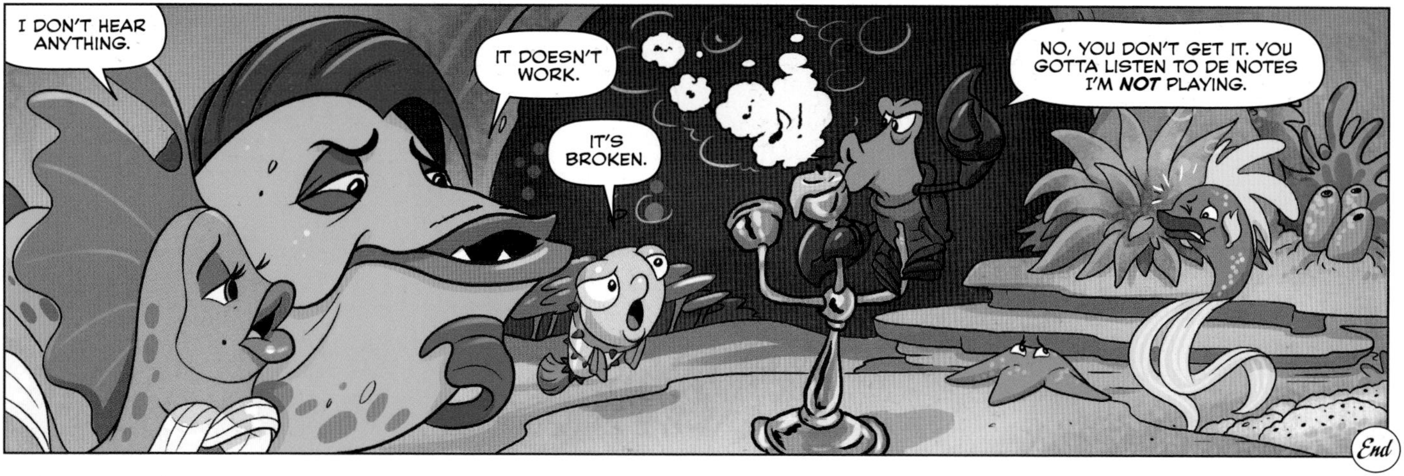
I DON'T HEAR ANYTHING.
IT DOESN'T WORK.
IT'S BROKEN.
NO, YOU DON'T GET IT. YOU GOTTA LISTEN TO DE NOTES I'M **NOT** PLAYING.
End

BELLE FEAST

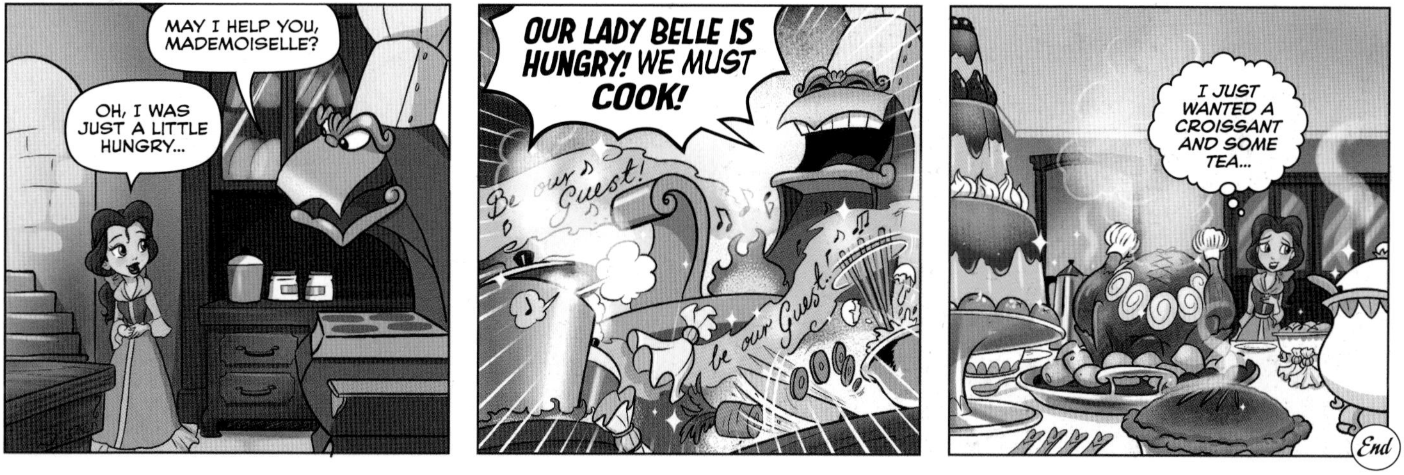
MAY I HELP YOU, MADEMOISELLE?
OH, I WAS JUST A LITTLE HUNGRY...
OUR LADY BELLE IS HUNGRY! WE MUST COOK!
Be our Guest!
be our Guest...
I JUST WANTED A CROISSANT AND SOME TEA...
End

DRYING DAY

WASH DAY...

HOUR THREE OF DRYING...

...THE CHAMELEON STILL FAILS TO BRING ME SNACKS.

End

LOUIS' FAN CLUB

ANOTHER GOOD NIGHT. THE NEW MENU IS A HIT!

BECAUSE MY WAITRESS IS A *GENIUS!*

OH, YOU! HAS THE BAND LEFT?

ALL EXCEPT *LOUIS.* HE, AH... HAS SOME *FANS* WAITING FOR HIM.

N-NOW YOU LADIES JUS' BACK OFF.

I DON' *WANNA* BE A PURSE!

End

BIRTHDAY MAGIC

YOUR BIRTHDAY IS COMING UP, DEAR. ARE YOU EXCITED?

OH, FATHER INSISTS ON A BANQUET. I KNOW PHILLIP IS HIDING GIFTS IN THE STABLES, BUT...

I'D BE HAPPY WITH A HOMEMADE DRESS AND CAKE FROM MY FAVORITE FAIRIES. JUST LIKE THE OLD DAYS IN THE FOREST!

A SIMPLE BIRTHDAY! NO FRILLS OR RICHES OR MAGIC.

NO MAGIC?

OH DEAR! FLORA, MERRYWEATHER! LISTEN TO WHAT AURORA TOLD ME.

SHE WANTS A BIRTHDAY DRESS AND CAKE, LIKE WE DID ON HER 16TH BIRTHDAY. AND SHE WANTS IT *WITHOUT* MAGIC!

OH MY, WE NEVER *DID* TELL HER WE USED OUR WANDS . . .

WELL THEN, WE'LL DO IT *RIGHT* THIS TIME. NO MAGIC, FOR AURORA!

YOU... CHOP FOOD WITH THESE, RIGHT?

YES, AFTER YOU THREAD THE FORKS.

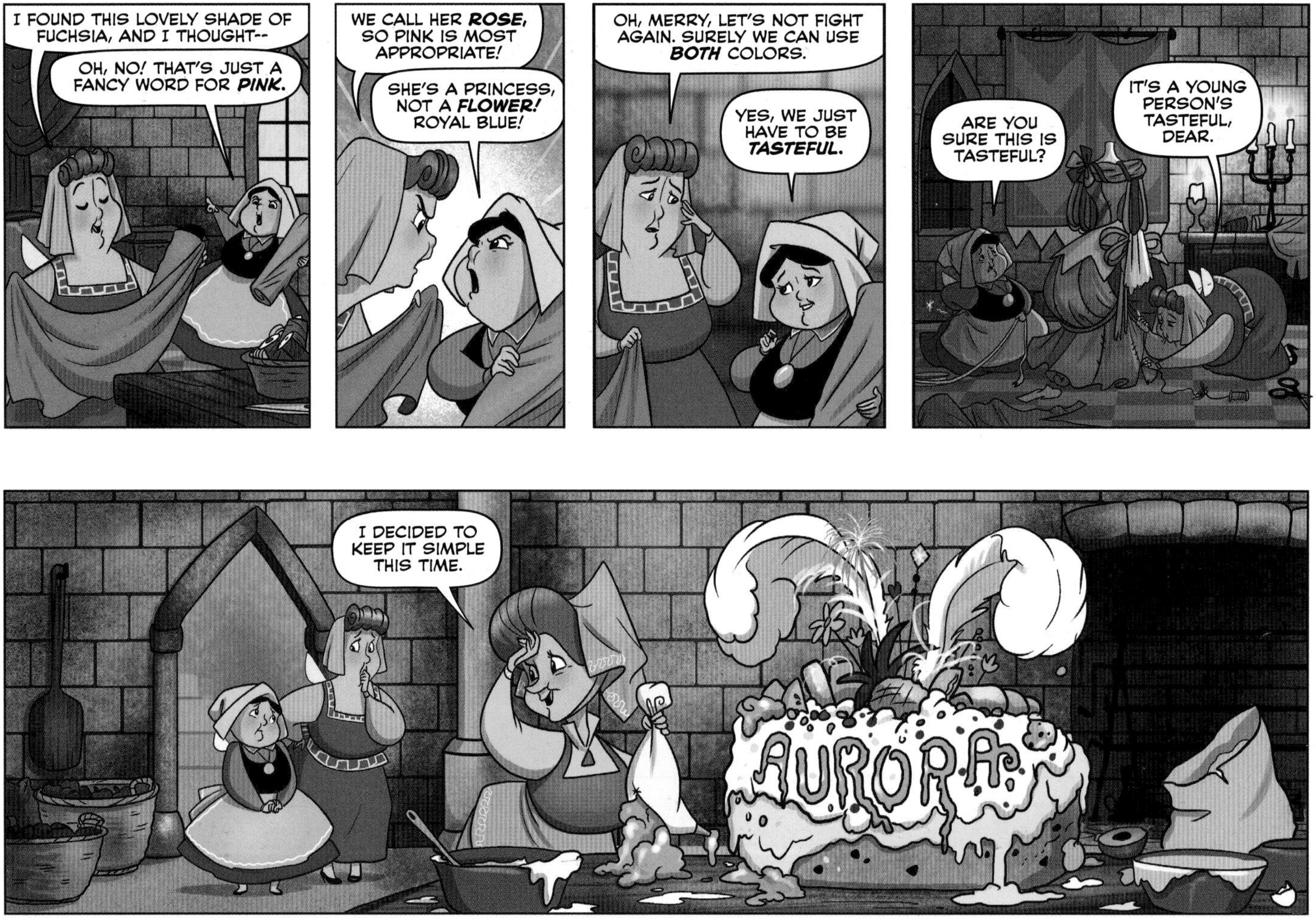
I FOUND THIS LOVELY SHADE OF FUCHSIA, AND I THOUGHT--
OH, NO! THAT'S JUST A FANCY WORD FOR **PINK.**
WE CALL HER **ROSE,** SO PINK IS MOST APPROPRIATE!
SHE'S A PRINCESS, NOT A **FLOWER!** ROYAL BLUE!
OH, MERRY, LET'S NOT FIGHT AGAIN. SURELY WE CAN USE **BOTH** COLORS.
YES, WE JUST HAVE TO BE **TASTEFUL.**
ARE YOU SURE THIS IS TASTEFUL?
IT'S A YOUNG PERSON'S TASTEFUL, DEAR.
I DECIDED TO KEEP IT SIMPLE THIS TIME.
AURORA

GOOD MORNING, PRINCESS.

HAPPY BIRTHDAY!!!

MY DARLINGS! THANK YOU!

WE MADE SOMETHING FOR YOU.

REALLY?! OH, SHOW ME!

!

WE DID OUR BEST, I'M SORR--

THEY'RE BEAUTIFUL!!!!

I CAN'T BELIEVE SHE'S WEARING OUR DRESS TO THE BANQUET!

I CAN'T TELL IF PHILLIP'S HAPPY OR TRYING NOT TO LAUGH.

LOOK, HERE COMES THE CAKE...

WHY IS THE SERVANT EATING HER CAKE?

ROYAL TASTER, DEAR. IT'S HIS JOB.

BLEEEECH

WELL, THE FROSTING IS DELICIOUS.

End

47

PRINCESS CHORES

DUTIES ARE NEVER DONE, EVEN FOR A PRINCESS.

CLOTHES ALWAYS NEED MENDING. SOCKS FIRST.

≥SIGH≤ WHY THE MICE **NEED** SOCKS, I'LL NEVER KNOW.

End

ENCHANTED ADJUSTMENTS

DO YOU LIKE YOUR LIBRARY, BELLE?

OF COURSE, I **LOVE** IT!

AND THE SERVANTS? THEIR...UH... **FORMS** AREN'T SCARING YOU?

NO...WELL, EXCEPT WHEN I DON'T **EXPECT** THEM.

≥AAAH! **MY BACK! CLOSE MEEE!**≤

EEK!

AH. THAT MUST BE JARVIS, THE LIBRARIAN.

NO MANNERS, THE CRANKY OLD COOT!

End

MERIDA, WE NEED TO DISCUSS THE CLAN BANQUET.

I KNOW, I'LL WATCH THE TRIPLETS.

I ALSO WANT YOU TO RECITE SOMETHING FOR ENTERTAINMENT. YOU NEED TO PRACTICE YOUR PUBLIC SPEAKING.

OH MUM, *WHAT?!*

DON'T FUSS, THE BANQUET NEEDS SOME REFINED ENTERTAINMENT. SOMETHING SOOTHING, GENTLE...

CAN I USE—

NO BATTLE-AXES, MERIDA.

MY LORDS, THE PRINCESS MERIDA WILL NOW RECITE FOR YOU.

⇒SIIIIIGH⇐

"O MY LUVE'S LIKE A RED, RED ROSE, THAT'S NEWLY SPRUNG IN JUNE;"

"O MY LUVE'S LIKE THE MELODIE, THAT'S SWEETLY PLAY'D IN TUNE."

WELL, I NEVER!

I THINK I LOST THEM AT "LUVE".

I'LL WAKE 'EM UP...≷AHEM≷

"AND EACH MAN FOUGHT HARD WITH MACE AND LANCE PELL MELL,"

EH?.. LANCE?

"AND THE RANKS WERE INSTANTLY FILLED UP AS SOON AS A MAN FELL;"

Z

"AND THE COUNT BOLDLY CHARGED THE BLACK PRINCE. AND CRIED, YIELD YOU, SIR KNIGHT, OR I'LL MAKE YOU WINCE!"

NOW *THAT'S* POETRY!

IT IS?

ADMIT IT, MUM, THEY ENJOYED *MY* POEM MORE THAN YOURS!

THEY DID AT THAT.

SO...IT'S PAST THE BOYS' BEDTIME AND I'M A LITTLE TIRED MYSELF...

VERY WELL, DEAR, YOU MAY RETIRE.

OKAY, NO MORE POETRY. TIME FOR THE *REAL* PARTY!

End

DEFENSIVE TRAINING

TODAY LET'S BRUSH UP ON DEFENSIVE TRAINING!

YOU WILL LEARN YOUR WEAK SPOTS AND HOW TO PROTECT THEM.

WEAK SPOTS? THE MIGHTY YAO HAS NO WEAK SPOTS! I AM A *WARRIOR!*

IT LOOKS LIKE THE MIGHTY YAO IS PLENTY DEFENSIVE ALREADY!

FEEL MY MIGHTY PINKIE!

ALL RIGHT, LING. COME AT ME AS HARD AS YOU CAN!

I DUNNO, MULAN, YOU'RE A FRIEND, I CAN'T ATTACK *YOU!*

I TOLD ALL THE GIRLS YOU SMELL LIKE FISH SAUCE!

YOU DID WHAT ARRGH!

FIRST RULE, LEAVE YOUR EGO IN YOUR TENT!

I BATHE, I SWEAR!

IF SOMEBODY COMES AT YOU WITH A RANGE WEAPON, THEY WILL HAVE MOMENTUM.

USE IT AGAINST THEM.

AVOID THE ATTACK AND DISORIENT THEM.

AND THAT'S HOW TO EXIT A BATTLE GRACEFULLY.

HE'S LIKE AN ANGRY SWAN, SO NICE.

DEFENSE IS ESPECIALLY IMPORTANT IN ARMED COMBAT.

THE BIGGER YOU ARE, THE MORE STRIKE POINTS YOU HAVE.

TOO MUCH ARMOR WILL SLOW YOU DOWN, SO YOU MUST MANEUVER.

YOU'RE SUPPOSED TO DEFEND YOURSELF.

YOU NEVER SAID HOW.

INTIMIDATION WILL SERVE YOU BY LOWERING YOUR ATTACKER'S CONFIDENCE. LOOK THEM IN THE EYES AND SPEAK FROM YOUR WARRIOR SOUL.

I WISH US AN HONORABLE BATTLE.

PREPARE TO JOIN YOUR ANCESTORS!

NOT THE FACE!

NOW LET'S PUT ALL OF THIS TRAINING INTO PRACTICE.

ATTACK!

SMASH

THOK

PAF!

oof

TNUT

AND WHAT HAVE WE LEARNED?

ONLY FIGHT THE FIGHTS YOU ABSOLUTELY MUST!

CLASS DISMISSED!

End

WAKE UP CALL

WELL, THAT'S *THREE* DAYS NOW EUGENE HAS SLEPT TOO LATE AND MISSED BREAKFAST.

GO TO PHASE TWO, PASCAL.

NYAAARGH!

DID I MISS BACON?

ALL GONE!

End

PRICELESS

A GIFT FROM KING HUBERT, YOUR HIGHNESS!

I BET THEY'RE BEAUTIFUL *ROSE-RED* RUBIES!

OH, NO NO-- *SAPPHIRES!* BLUE AS THE OCEAN!

FANCY THAT! EMERALDS!

End

OUTRAGEOUS! I WON'T GO! I'LL LOCK MYSELF IN MY CHAMBERS AND NEVER COME OUT!

?!

WHAT IS IT?

READ FOR YOURSELF.

THIS IS JUST A MEMO FROM THE GRAND DUKE NOTIFYING YOU OF A COUNCIL MEETING.

THERE GOES MY BIRD-WATCHING CLUB!

WHY SHOULDN'T THE GRAND DUKE INVITE YOU TO A COUNCIL MEETING? ISN'T IT YOUR DUTY TO ATTEND?

COUNCIL MEETINGS ARE SUCH A NUISANCE!

ALL THE DUKE WANTS TO DISCUSS ARE BORING THINGS, LIKE CIVIC EVENTS AND IMPROVEMENTS TO KINGDOM ROADS.

AND HE'LL JUST GO ON AND ON AND ON...WHAT A TIRESOME WINDBAG.

PERHAPS HE MIGHT SAY THE SAME THING ABOUT YOU?

IMPOSSIBLE! I'M A PERFECT DELIGHT!

PERHAPS I COULD COME ALONG TO YOUR MEETING AND PROVIDE SOME HELPFUL HINTS ON HOW TO SPEED THINGS ALONG?

OH MY DEAR, THAT'D BE SPLENDID!

FOR INSTANCE, THINGS MIGHT MOVE FASTER IF YOU PAY ATTENTION SO THE GRAND DUKE DOESN'T HAVE TO REPEAT HIMSELF.

WHAT WAS THAT, CINDERELLA?

I SAID MEETINGS GO FASTER WHEN--

SON, GUESS WHAT? CINDERELLA IS GOING TO COME TO MY MEETING AND SOLVE ALL OF MY PROBLEMS FOR ME!

SPLENDID!

GOOD AFTERNOON! IT'S SUCH A..*PLEASURE* TO BE HERE. LET'S GET THIS CIVIC COUNCIL MEETING UNDERWAY.

I LISTENED, DIDN'T I? YOU'D NEVER KNOW I WAS COMPLAINING ABOUT THE DUKE AND ALL HIS RIDICULOUS FOL-DE-ROL YESTERDAY!

NO ONE *WOULD* HAVE KNOWN...

...IF THE GRAND DUKE WASN'T SITTING RIGHT NEXT TO YOU.

MY DEAR GRAND DUKE! I FORGOT YOU WERE SITTING THERE, HOW DID THAT HAPPEN?

NO OFFENSE TAKEN, YOUR HIGHNESS. AFTER ALL...

...I CAN'T HELP THINKING THAT THESE MEETINGS MIGHT GO MORE SMOOTHLY *WITHOUT* YOUR ROYAL PRESENCE.

CINDERELLA! TELL HIM I'M A PERFECT DELIGHT!

THE NEXT MORNING...

AFTER YESTERDAY'S EVENTS, MAYBE I COULD OFFER SOME ADVICE ON BEING A MORE GRACIOUS MEETING ATTENDEE?

YOUNG LADY, I'VE BEEN A KING A LOT LONGER THAN YOU'VE BEEN A PRINCESS. I THINK I KNOW MORE ABOUT THESE THINGS THAN YOU DO.

WELL...LET'S SAY YOUR MIND WANDERED WHILE SOMEONE WAS TALKING. WHAT WOULD YOU DO?

EASY! I'D INTERRUPT AT ONCE AND START TALKING ABOUT MYSELF.

CLASS BEGINS NOW.

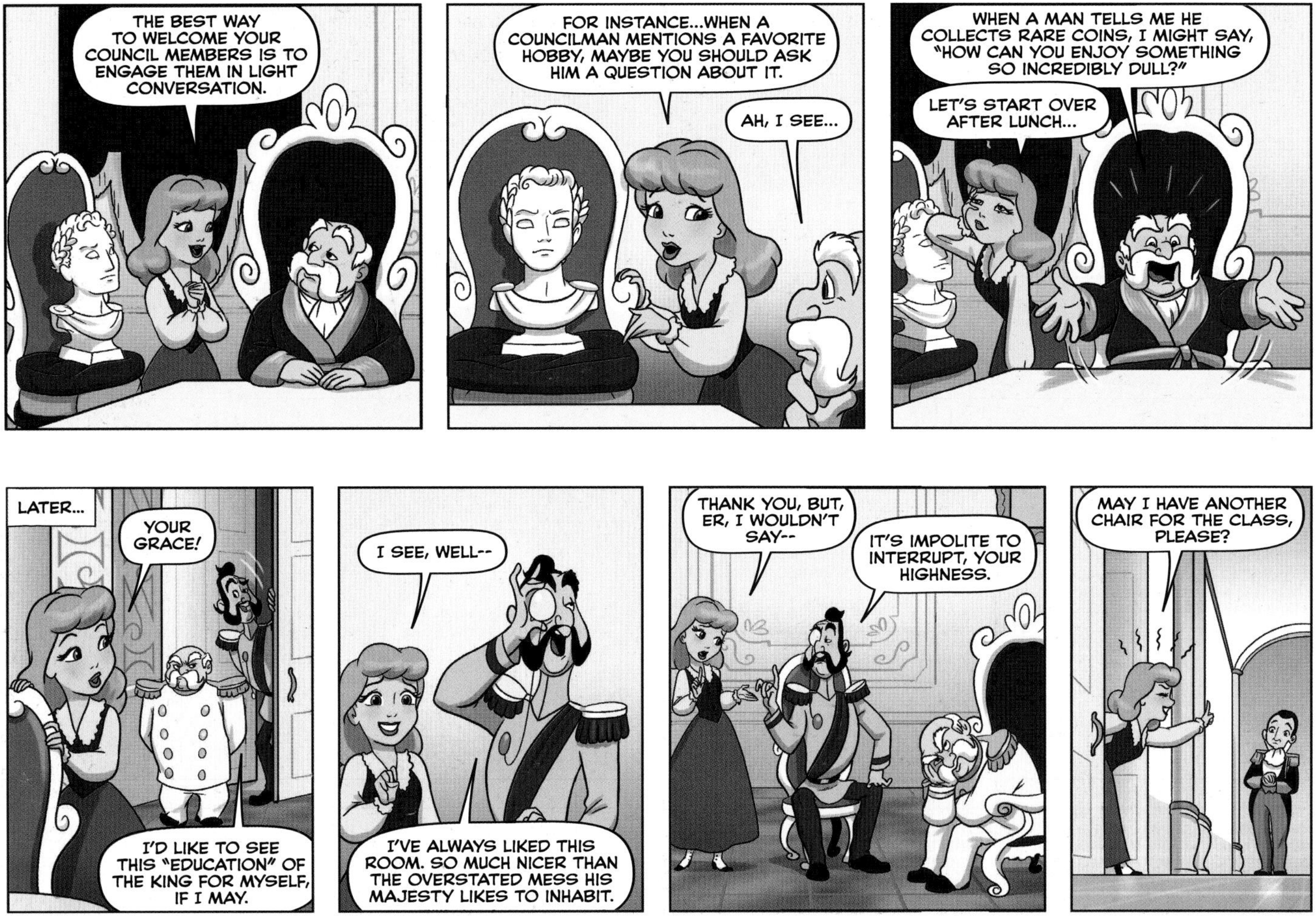
THE BEST WAY TO WELCOME YOUR COUNCIL MEMBERS IS TO ENGAGE THEM IN LIGHT CONVERSATION.
FOR INSTANCE...WHEN A COUNCILMAN MENTIONS A FAVORITE HOBBY, MAYBE YOU SHOULD ASK HIM A QUESTION ABOUT IT.
AH, I SEE...
WHEN A MAN TELLS ME HE COLLECTS RARE COINS, I MIGHT SAY, "HOW CAN YOU ENJOY SOMETHING SO INCREDIBLY DULL?"
LET'S START OVER AFTER LUNCH...
LATER...
YOUR GRACE!
I'D LIKE TO SEE THIS "EDUCATION" OF THE KING FOR MYSELF, IF I MAY.
I SEE, WELL--
I'VE ALWAYS LIKED THIS ROOM. SO MUCH NICER THAN THE OVERSTATED MESS HIS MAJESTY LIKES TO INHABIT.
THANK YOU, BUT, ER, I WOULDN'T SAY--
IT'S IMPOLITE TO INTERRUPT, YOUR HIGHNESS.
MAY I HAVE ANOTHER CHAIR FOR THE CLASS, PLEASE?

IT'S ESSENTIAL IN A POLITE CONVERSATION NOT TO INTERRUPT. LET'S TRY IT.

THE WEATHER HAS BEEN UNSEASONABLY WARM, DON'T YOU THINK?

YES, I--

IT HAS! HOWEVER--

THE SUN HAS BEEN GOOD FOR THE CROPS. DON'T YOU AGREE?

WELL, I--

IT HAS INDEED!

HOW FANTASTIC IT FEELS *NOT* TO BE INTERRUPTED!

QUITE SO! YOU SHOULD TRY IT SOMETIME, YOUR HIGHNESS.

HOW ARE THE LESSONS GOING, CINDERELLA?

OH, I CAN'T CHANGE THE KING OR THE GRAND DUKE. THEY'RE HAPPY THE WAY THEY ARE.

BUT MY *NEW* STUDENT HAS COME *SUCH* A LONG WAY!

NEW STUDENT? WHO--?

TWO LUMPS, IF YOU PLEAZY.

AND S'MORE CHEEZY?

MYERR!

End

BIRD SONGS

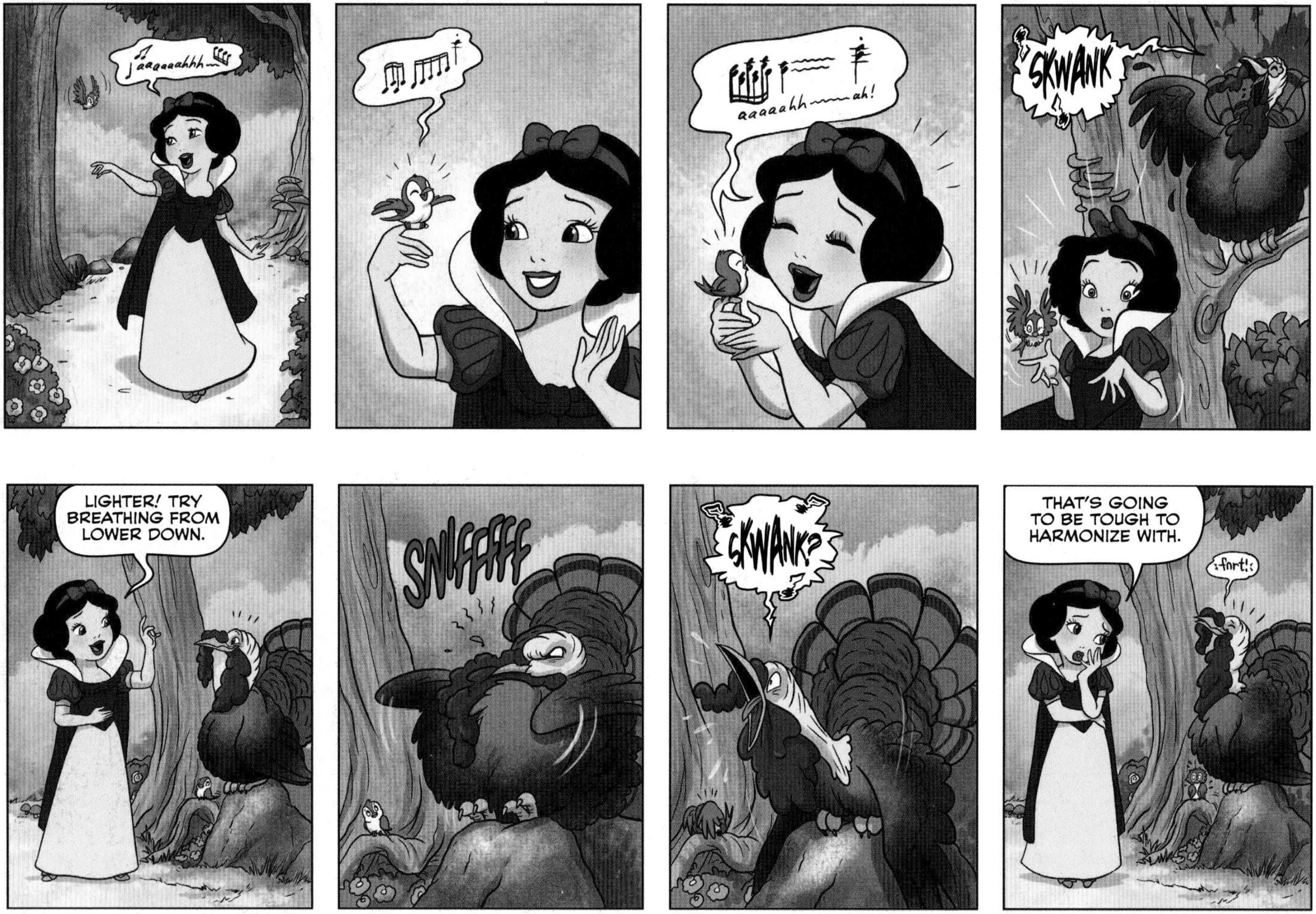
aaaaaaahhh
aaaaahh—ah!
SKWANK
LIGHTER! TRY BREATHING FROM LOWER DOWN.
SNIFFFFF
SKWANK?
THAT'S GOING TO BE TOUGH TO HARMONIZE WITH.
fart!

♪ ♫

THAT'S IT! I THINK WE'VE GOT IT!

WHO?

A *BARITONE!* HOW SPLENDID!

YOU KEEP RHYTHM ON TWO AND FOUR, AND YOU HOLD THE LONG HIGH NOTES.

IF YOU CAN HANDLE BASS, I THINK THIS LITTLE FELLOW WILL BE A GREAT TREBLE.

AND YOU...

KEEP UP THE GOOD WORK. REMEMBER, LESS IS MORE!

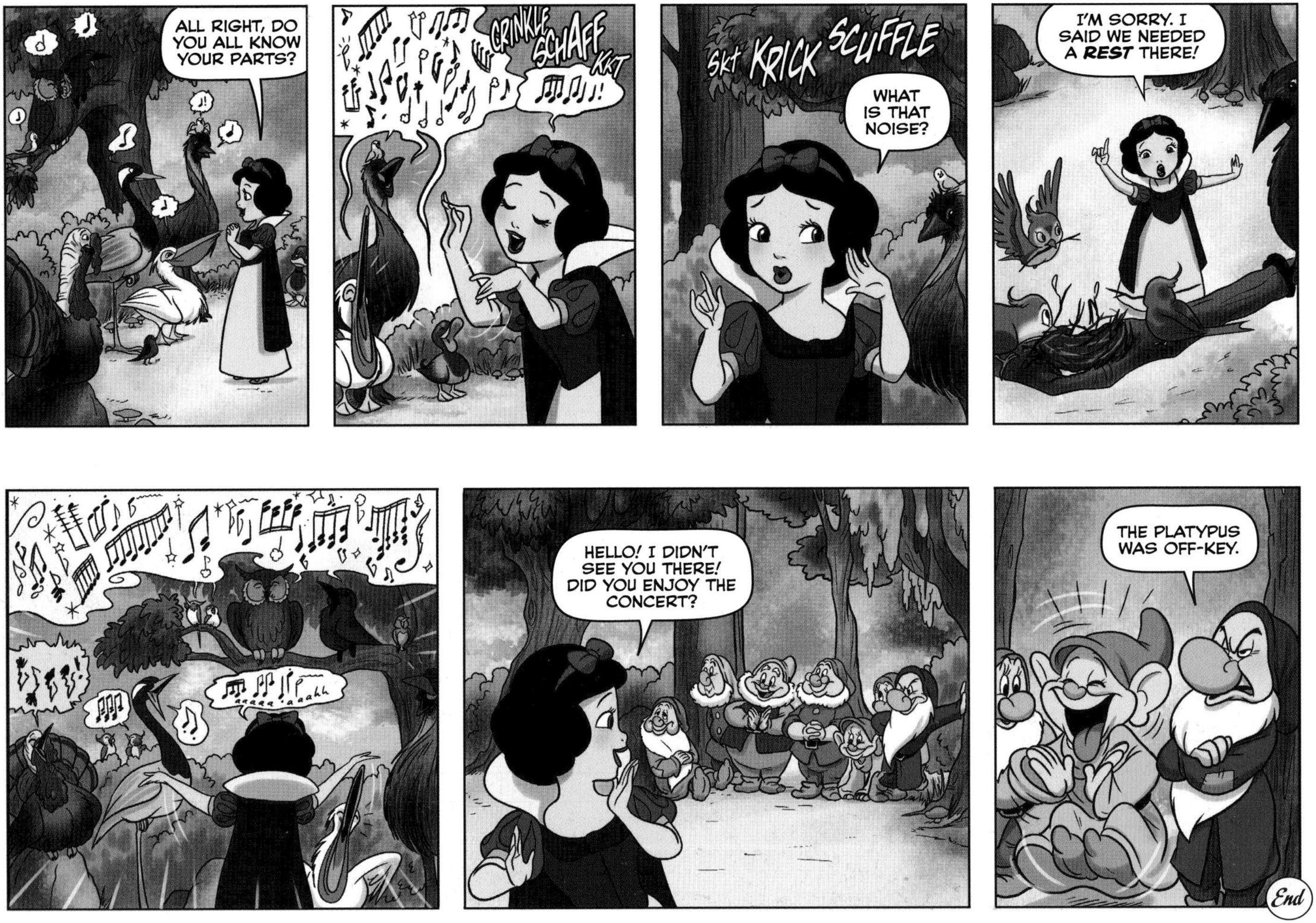
ALL RIGHT, DO YOU ALL KNOW YOUR PARTS?
CRINKLE
SCHAFF
KKT
SKT
KRICK
SCUFFLE
WHAT IS THAT NOISE?
I'M SORRY. I SAID WE NEEDED A **REST** THERE!
aaaaa aaahh
HELLO! I DIDN'T SEE YOU THERE! DID YOU ENJOY THE CONCERT?
THE PLATYPUS WAS OFF-KEY.
End

BELLE'S DILEMMA

MAM'SELLE, WHY YOU ALWAYS SIT IN *ZIS* CHAIR? WE 'AVE SO MANY!

WELL, I LIKE IT BECAUSE IT'S... PRIVATE.

CACHÉ, MAM'SELLE?

OH I JUST MEAN THAT... WELL...

WHEN YOU LIVE WITH ENCHANTED OBJECTS THAT CAN HEAR AND SEE EVERYTHING YOU DO, SOMETIMES YOU NEED SOME... TIME ALONE, YOU KNOW?

OUI OUI, I UNDERSTAND *ABSOLUMENT!*

EVERYBODY OUT! *TOUT DE SUITE!*

AWWW...

'SCUSE ME, MISS, YOU'RE ON MY TASSELS.

AHH, FINALLY SOME PEACE AND PRIVACY...

AH!

'ULLO!

I DON'T BELIEVE THIS, AN ENCHANTED *BOOKMARK?*

KEEP GOING, YOU'RE NEARLY AT THE BIT WHERE--

SPOILERS.

OW!

I'LL TAKE THAT, CHILD, YOU JUST RELAX.

ALLOW ME! GOOD NIGHT, MISS BELLE.

ER... THANK YOU.

SO, TONIGHT YOU WILL BE WEARING THIS LOVELY YELLOW PEIGNOIR WITH THE FINEST SPANISH LACE...

I HOPE MY DREAMS AREN'T PICKED FOR ME...

AND NOW, THE QUARTET WILL PLAY 'PERSIAN DREAMSCAPE'

I NEED TO TALK TO YOU.

WHA?

I DON'T MEAN TO SOUND RUDE, BECAUSE I KNOW EVERYONE MEANS WELL...

WHAT HAPPENED?

I JUST...DON'T NEED EVERYTHING DONE FOR ME! IT'S DRIVING ME CRAZY!

I'M NOT SURE I--

I WENT TO SCRATCH MY NOSE. LUMIERE TRIED TO HELP AND ALMOST SCORCHED MY HAIR!

I'LL TALK TO THEM.

I WANT TO POLITELY REMIND EVERYONE THAT BELLE DOES NOT NEED ATTENDING TO *ALL* OF THE TIME. IN FACT, SHE FINDS IT A BIT STIFLING.

WELL! HOW UNGRATEFUL. WE'RE TREATING HER LIKE A *PRINCESS.*

BUT SHE EEZ *NOT* A PRINCESS, SHE EEZ NOT USED TO ZIS ATTENTION!

I CAN'T LET THE POOR CHILD *WORK*, SHE'S NOT A SERVANT!

DO YOU *WANT* A TRUE LOVE WITH ROUGH, CHAPPED HANDS, SIRE?

WHY ON *EARTH* WOULD I CARE ABOUT *THAT??*

GOOD POINT, SIRE, CONSIDERING SHE DOESN'T SEEM TO MIND YOUR... AROMA.

NO NO NO...!

THERE IS *PROTOCOL* TO OBSERVE!

WE'RE JUST DOING OUR JOB!

GRRRR...

SILENCE!

WHAM

SHLUMPNFLORCH

OH NO, HER *BOOKS...*

OOOH, CHAUCER IS HEAVY!

THIS WILL NOT DO! I CANNOT LIFT BOOKS!

NONE OF US CAN, WE'RE TOO SMALL!

I'LL DO IT!

PERFECT TOUCH, SIRE.

WELL I DON'T KNOW HOW THEY WERE BEFORE!

≥AHEM≤

MAY I BE OF ASSISTANCE?

OH MY DEAR, WE'RE SO SORRY ABOUT ALL THIS MESS!

DON'T BE SORRY!

YOU'VE ALL BEEN SO KIND TO ME AND I'M VERY GRATEFUL. LET ME HELP YOU, NOW.

I'M REALLY NOT SUITED TO A LIFE OF LUXURY. I'M JUST A GIRL LOOKING FOR ADVENTURE.

AND RIGHT NOW, ADVENTURES NEED SORTING!

CHAUCER FIRST!

End

YOU WANT TO **WHAT**, LOTTIE?

IT'S THE **MODERN** WAY, TIANA! I INVITE ALL THE ELIGIBLE MEN TO CONVINCE **ME** WHY THEY'RE WORTHY OF MY ATTENTIONS!

SOUNDS LIKE WHEN YOU SHOP FOR SHOES!

YES! EXCEPT GENTLEMEN DON'T GIVE YOU BLISTERS!

WELL IF YOU'RE GONNA TRY THIS, YOU TRY IT HERE IN THE RESTAURANT, OKAY?

OH TIA, YOU'RE A **PEACH**, THANK YOU!!

ORDER EXTRA CLEAN TABLECLOTHS, LOTTIE THROWS DRINKS.

OH. I KNOW.

OH TIA, IT ALL LOOKS SIMPLY MAHVELOUS!

DON'T THANK ME YET. I'M GOING TO CHAPERONE EVERY ONE OF YOUR DATES.

AND JUST WHAT MAKES YOU THINK I CAN'T JUDGE FOR MYSELF?

I'M LEARNING CURSIVE, SO I CAN WRITE LOVE LETTERS NOW!

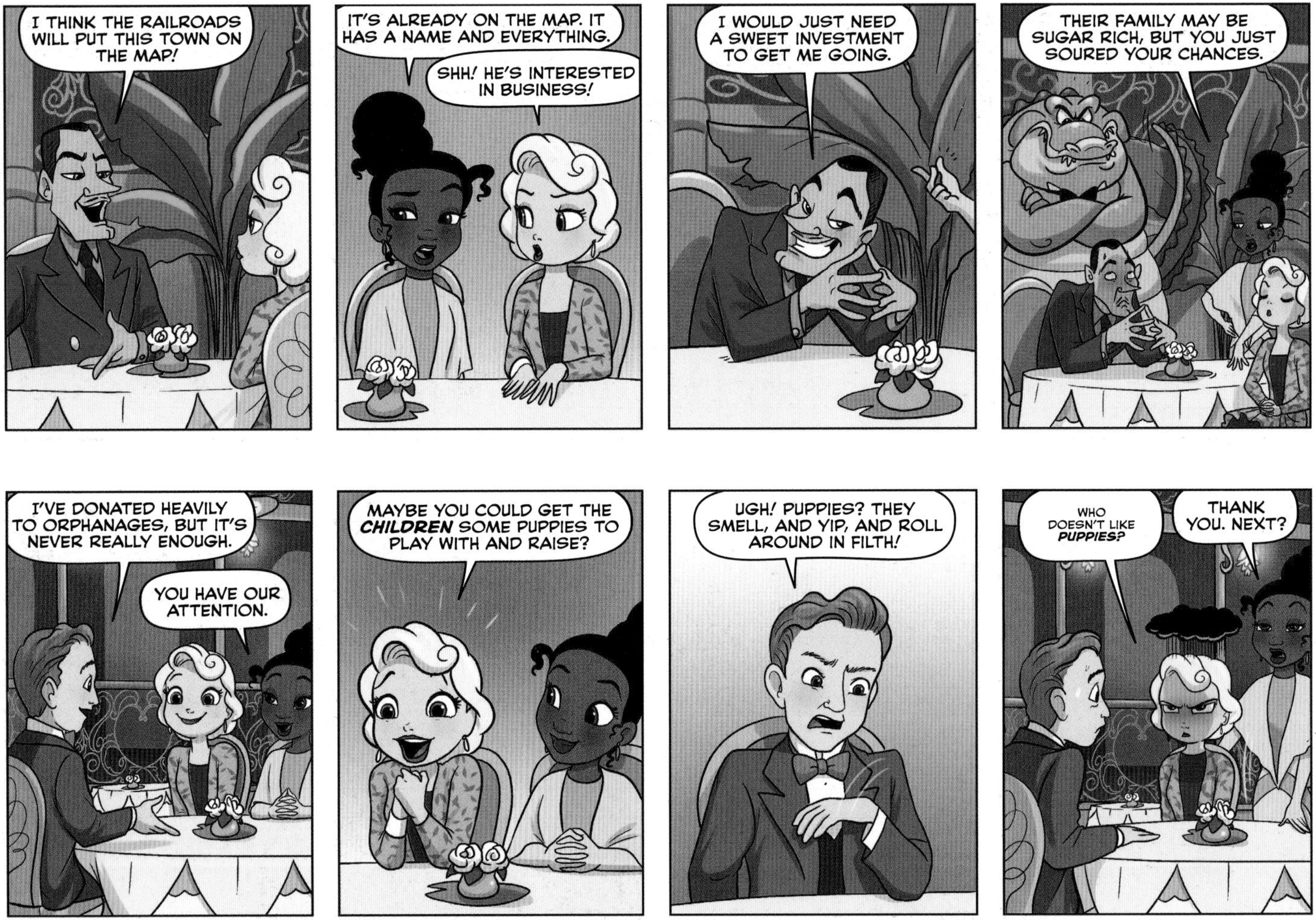
I THINK THE RAILROADS WILL PUT THIS TOWN ON THE MAP!
IT'S ALREADY ON THE MAP. IT HAS A NAME AND EVERYTHING.
SHH! HE'S INTERESTED IN BUSINESS!
I WOULD JUST NEED A SWEET INVESTMENT TO GET ME GOING.
THEIR FAMILY MAY BE SUGAR RICH, BUT YOU JUST SOURED YOUR CHANCES.
I'VE DONATED HEAVILY TO ORPHANAGES, BUT IT'S NEVER REALLY ENOUGH.
YOU HAVE OUR ATTENTION.
MAYBE YOU COULD GET THE ***CHILDREN*** SOME PUPPIES TO PLAY WITH AND RAISE?
UGH! PUPPIES? THEY SMELL, AND YIP, AND ROLL AROUND IN FILTH!
WHO DOESN'T LIKE ***PUPPIES?***
THANK YOU. NEXT?

SO TELL US A LITTLE BIT ABOUT YOURSELF.

WELL I WAS RAISED UP IN THE NORTHEAST, ATTENDED ONLY THE FINEST SCHOOLS, WHERE I WAS TRAINED IN FENCING AND HORSE RIDING. NOT AT SAME TIME, MIND YOU! WOULD BE TOO DANG...

...AND WE WENT ON AN ADVENTURE TO THE CONGO, WHERE I LEARNED FOURTEEN LANGUAGES. I CAN ALSO PILOT SMALL AIRCRAFT AND AM NOT TERRIBLE AT BOATING. I CAN...

AND I'M AN EXCELLENT LISTENER!

WAKE UP! I THINK HE'S WRAPPING UP!

Z

IT'S SO NICE TO SEE YOU AGAIN, LOTTIE!

AGAIN?

THIS IS TRAVIS.

TRAVIS?

YOU MET AT THE BALL. AND THEN THE PARADE.

AND MY GRAND OPENING.

????

WHAT A LOVELY...UM...

NAPKIN. YOU HAVE ONE, TOO.

I THINK THAT MAY HAVE BEEN EVERY ELIGIBLE MAN IN TOWN.

I CAN SEE WHY.

WHAT DOES A SUGAR BARON'S DAUGHTER HAVE TO DO TO FIND A LITTLE **ARM CANDY?**

LIKE I TELL MY CUSTOMERS, IF YOU DON'T LIKE THE MENU, YOU DON'T HAVE TO ORDER.

YOU DON'T NEED A BOYFRIEND TO GO ON TRIPS, GET SOME READING DONE, GO DANCING--

THANK YOU!

End

RAINY DAY

TIME TO RISE AND SHINE, PASCAL! IT'S A NEW DAY!

FLING

TIME TO LET SOME LIGHT IN!

KRA-KOOM

...THIRTY MILLION VOLTS OF IT!

PHEW, WELL **THIS** IS GOING TO TAKE A LITTLE MORE THAN THE USUAL MOP AND SHINE-UP!

I MEAN, THAT'S THE SNEAKIEST DOWNPOUR I'VE EVER SEEN! I ONLY HAD THE WINDOW OPEN FOR A SECOND!

ONLY ONE THING FOR THIS, PASCAL!

TIME FOR THE **EMERGENCY** MOP!

PHEW, ALL DONE AND IT'S ONLY 7:20!

OH NO. NO NO NO, THE CEILING'S **LEAKING** NOW?

DWOP

QUICK, QUICK, NEED SOMETHING TO CATCH IT IN....

COOKING FOR ONLY TWO PEOPLE, WE WORK WITH WHAT WE'VE GOT!

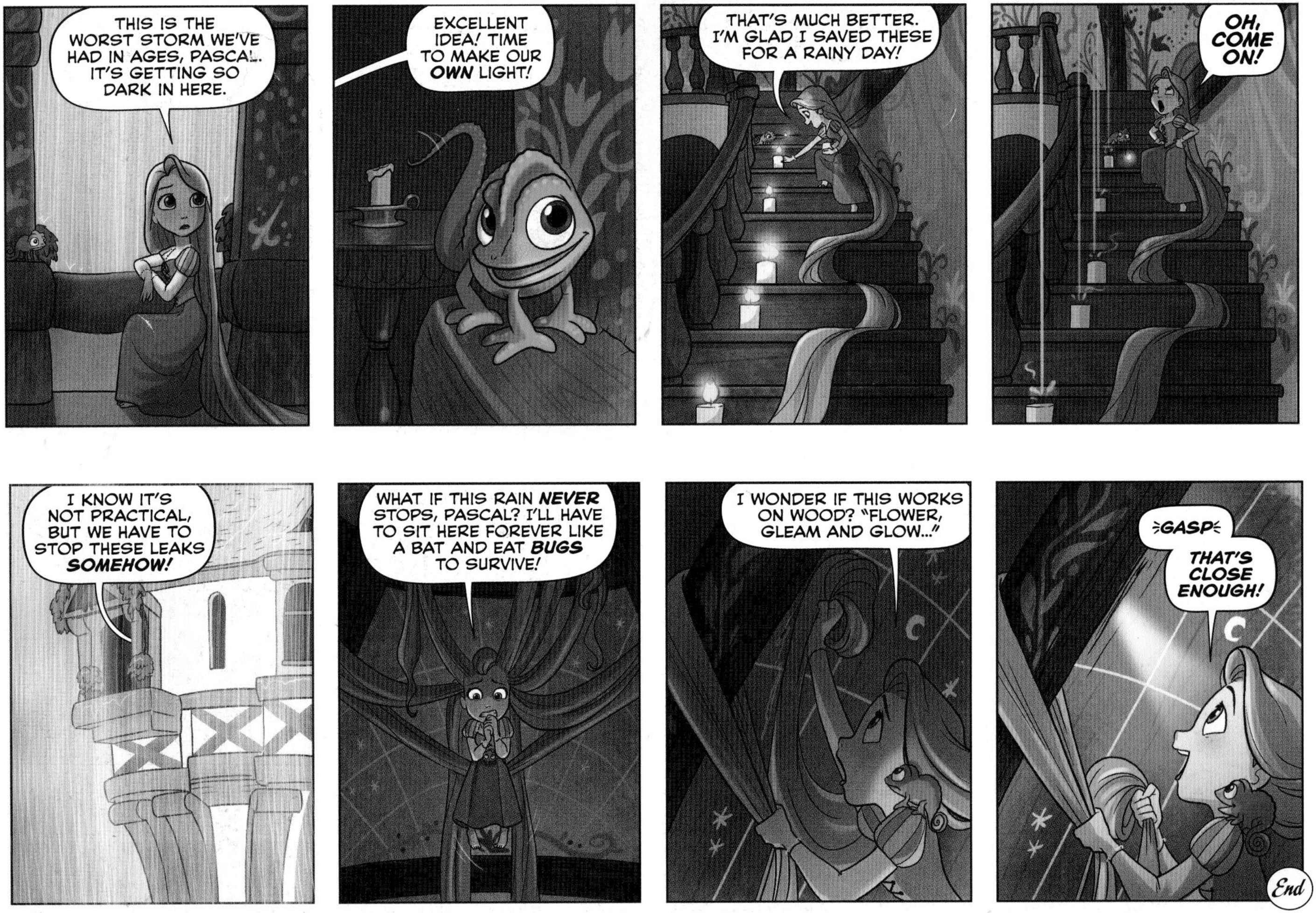
THIS IS THE WORST STORM WE'VE HAD IN AGES, PASCAL. IT'S GETTING SO DARK IN HERE.
EXCELLENT IDEA! TIME TO MAKE OUR OWN LIGHT!
THAT'S MUCH BETTER. I'M GLAD I SAVED THESE FOR A RAINY DAY!
OH, COME ON!
I KNOW IT'S NOT PRACTICAL, BUT WE HAVE TO STOP THESE LEAKS SOMEHOW!
WHAT IF THIS RAIN NEVER STOPS, PASCAL? I'LL HAVE TO SIT HERE FOREVER LIKE A BAT AND EAT BUGS TO SURVIVE!
I WONDER IF THIS WORKS ON WOOD? "FLOWER, GLEAM AND GLOW..."
GASP
THAT'S CLOSE ENOUGH!
End

A HOT ARABIAN NIGHT.

GOOD RAJAH. THERE'S YOUR TIGER PILLOW, RIGHT OVER THERE.

OOOF! NO, RAJAH, *DOWN*. TIGER PILLOW! TIGER PILLOW!

I CAN'T FEEL MY LEGS!!

PURRRR...

RAJAH, YOU ARE *TOO HEAVY* TO SLEEP ON MY LEGS.

PURRRR...

LOOK, RAJAH. A BIRDIE!

RAWWWR?

GO GET IT!

PURRRR...

OKAY. *PLEASE* GET IT?

RAJAH, NO PLAYING. **SLEEP.**

IF YOU WANT TO STAY UP HERE, **SETTLE DOWN.**

OKAY, THAT'S BETTER. WE CAN SHARE THE BED. SHARE...

TEN MINUTES LATER.

FIRST THING TOMORROW, I WILL FIND A NEW TIGER TRAINER.

JASMINE?

JASMINE? JASMINE, WHERE ARE MY SPARE TURBAN FEATHERS? LET ME REMIND YOU THEY ARE **NOT** TIGER TOYS--

JASMINE?! RAJAH, WHAT'S THAT IN YOUR MOUTH?

?

YOU ATE MY JASMINE?!

HOW CAN I SLEEP WITH ALL THIS NONSENSE?

WHILE JASMINE SLEEPS OUTSIDE...

GUARDS! GUARDS!!!

GRRR?

RAJAH, I COMMAND YOU TO OPEN YOUR MOUTH AT ONCE!

?

DEAREST? ARE YOU IN THERE?

RAAWWWR... RAAWWWWW'R!

POOR JASMINE. SHE'S GONE ABSOLUTELY *FERAL*.

???

THE SULTAN THINKS RAJAH *ATE* PRINCESS JASMINE!

RAJAH, I ORDER YOU TO COUGH UP THE PRINCESS THIS INSTANCE.

DID YOU HEAR ME, YOU GROWLING PILE OF PILLOWS? COUGH HER UP *NOW!*

GRRRRRR!

WHEN IT COMES TO TIGERS, *DISCIPLINE* IS THE KEY--

SNARP

DISCIPLINE, AND PERHAPS A STRONGER PAIR OF PANTS.

COUGH UP MY DAUGHTER, YOU BEAST!

GRRROWWWR!

WOULD YOU PLEASE KEEP THE NOISE DOWN? I'M TRYING TO SLEEP!

THANK YOU!

WELL, I... SUPPOSE WE'RE *ALL* A LITTLE TO BLAME HERE, RIGHT RAJAH?

GRRRR!

ZZZZ...

SIGHHHH...

There's only **ONE** way to settle this...

GRRRMPH...

So soft, I don't need a pillow!

End

EXPLORING THE CASTLE

What's wrong, dear?

I'm just realizing how huge this castle is! I don't know where to start exploring.

Why not the basement? Then we can work our way up! It's right this way!

No no, the basement is to the south.

We've been away a while, too, haven't we?

IT'S SO DARK DOWN THERE. ARE YOU SURE IT'S SAFE?

NONSENSE! DARKNESS OR NOT, THIS IS YOUR HOME, WHERE YOU'RE *PERFECTLY* SAFE!

CRRREEEAAK

WHAT WAS THAT NOISE?

MERRYWEATHER'S HEART POUNDING.

I'M NOT SCARED. I'M JUST *TERRIFIED!*

WHAT IS THAT ROOM?

I DON'T KNOW. WE HAVE NEVER VENTURED THIS FAR DOWN.

WANDS UP! WE DON'T WANT ANY SURPRISES!

FATHER?!?

WELL, THERE GOES THE LAST QUIET ROOM IN THE KINGDOM!

End

KEKATA IS GOING TO ANOINT THE WARRIORS TONIGHT IN A SECRET CEREMONY!

I KNOW. FATHER WANTS ME TO GO, TO DRAW THE CORN CIRCLES.

YOU ARE SO LUCKY!

IT'S JUST TO ASK AHONE TO SOOTHE THE HEARTS OF THE WARRIORS AFTER THE BATTLE.

BUT *AFTER* THAT, THE MEN WILL DANCE AND THERE'LL BE THE FEAST...

YOU'RE RIGHT, I GUESS IT WON'T BE TOO BAD.

...AND YOU'LL SIT NEXT TO *KOCOUM.* ≥SIIGH≥

OH. I'M SO EXCITED.

OH. HELLO, KOCOUM.

WINGAPO, POCAHONTAS.

...SO. READY FOR A WELL-DESERVED PARTY?

I LOOK FORWARD TO SLEEPING WITHOUT THE CALL OF THE DRUMS.

OH COME NOW...YOU CAN AFFORD TO, UM...CUT LOOSE A BIT! YOU'VE EARNED IT.

"CUT LOOSE"?

I'M WEARING MY WOLFS-EYE AMULET, IS THAT NOT ENOUGH?

THIS'LL BE A LONG NIGHT...

AHONE SMILES UPON YOU ALL AND BIDS YOU PEACE. NOW LET US REJOICE IN OUR VICTORY!

SO HELP ME, MR. SERIOUS, I *WILL* GET YOU TO LAUGH TONIGHT!

KOCOUM, WANT TO SEE SOMETHING FUNNY?

WHAT ARE YOU DOING?

EMBARRASSING MYSELF, APPARENTLY...

MY, KOCOUM, WHAT A MAGNIFICENT BUCKSKIN CAPE!

THANK YOU. I WON IT IN BATTLE.

WHAT A COINCIDENCE! I WAS IN A BATTLE ONCE AND GOT A FINE HAT FOR IT! LET ME SHOW YOU!

BOO!

THE BATTLE FOR THE LEFTOVERS, I ASSUME?

OKAY, SO I LOST...

80

KOCOUM, I CREATED A SPECIAL DANCE JUST FOR YOU, NOW WATCH!

THIS IS THE TALE OF A PROUD HERON WHO WAS ALWAYS TALL AND STIFF AND RIGID AS THE REEDS!

ONE DAAAY.. THE *WIND* CAME TO VISIT! SHE BLEW ALL THROUGH HIS LONG SLICK FEATHERS....

...AND *TICKLED HIM!*

I AM NOT ITCHY, BUT I DO NEED A NEW DRINK.

I DON'T UNDERSTAND. HOW CAN SOMEONE NEVER EVER LAUGH?

HE *IS* A GREAT WARRIOR, THOUGH. HE HAS THE RESPECT AND ADMIRATION OF THE WHOLE TRIBE.

HRMMPPPHH...

HAHAHAHAHAHA!

MEEKO, KOCOUM IS NOW THE LAUGHING WARRIOR.

BUT THAT'S OUR LITTLE SECRET!

End

TOUGH CHOICES

WHAT TO READ NEXT, LET'S SEE...

I CAN READ THE TITLES TO YOU!

NO, I'M GONNA CHOOSE AT RANDOM! HERE GOES!

AHA! IT IS DECIDED!

'A HISTORY OF GREAT FRENCH HINGES', OOOH!

AW, I WAS HOPING FOR *THE LITTLE PRINCE...*

End

ARCHERY FORM

THE MOST IMPORTANT PART OF ARCHERY IS PROPER FORM.

THAT SO?

?!

TWANG

WHAT D'YE KNOW, BULL'S-EYE!

SEE? FORM.

End

I THINK I'VE GOTTEN THE HANG OF THIS WHOLE "BE A MAN" THING.

WELL, YOUR MAN STRUT LOOKS SOLID. I'LL GIVE YOU THAT!

DEEPEN YOUR VOICE. BELCH EVERY ONCE IN AWHILE. WHAT ELSE IS THERE?

OOF!

WHOAAA! LOOKS LIKE WE FOUND CHIEN-PO A NEW *ARM WRESTLING* OPPONENT...

YOU WERE SAYING?

ARG!

GRRRR!

AW, DON'T FEEL BAD FOR GIVING UP.

I *DIDN'T* GIVE UP!

CHIEN-PO HEARD THE DINNER GONG.

HE LOST SO MANY TIMES, SO QUICKLY.

HIS HANDS WERE SO SOFT.

WHAT KINDA *MAN* IS HE?

I CAN'T BELIEVE MY COVER IS GOING TO BE BLOWN BY SOMETHING AS IDIOTIC AS ARM WRESTLING!

NOT TO WORRY, MULAN. FOR YOU SEE, I AM AN ARM WRESTLING MASTER...

AND I WILL TRAIN YOU.

YOU'RE AN ARM WRESTLING MASTER? BUT YOUR ARMS ARE AS THIN AS CHOW MEIN NOODLES.

OH, COME ON! THEY'RE *AT LEAST* A LO MEIN.

OKAY, GIVE ME EVERYTHING YOU'VE GOT, MULAN. DON'T HOLD BACK!

WAIT, I WASN'T READY!

ALRIGHT, LET'S TRY IT AGAIN, *WHEN I'M READY* THIS TIME.

...AAAAAAND *BEGIN!*

WAIT, THERE WAS SOMETHING IN MY EYE! THAT LAST ONE DOESN'T COUNT!

ARM WRESTLING IS ABOUT MORE THAN DUMB STRENGTH. IT'S ABOUT THE SOPHISTICATED USE OF *PSYCHOLOGY.*

READY... SET...AND AWAY WE *GO!*

YOU LOOK RIDICULOUS.

RIDICULOU-*THHH AND* VICTORIOU-*THHH!*

YOU'VE GOTTA USE EVERY TRICK AT YOUR DISPOSAL TO WIN A MATCH.

READY... SET...LET IT *GO!*

PING! ONE HUNDRED PUSHUPS, NOW!

YES CAPTAIN SHANG!

THAT'S NOT VERY SPORTING.

ARM WRESTLING ISN'T A SPORT, MULAN. IT'S *WAR!*

YOUR TRAINING IS ALMOST COMPLETE. YOU HAVE ONE MORE TECHNIQUE TO LEARN, WHICH IS SURE TO DISTRACT ANY OPPONENT.

BREATHING FIRE!

LIKE *THIS!*

≥COUGH≤

THAT MAY WORK BETTER ON SPICY NOODLES NIGHT.

I'LL GRAB YOU SOME SZECHUAN PEPPER.

THE NEXT DAY...

I'D LIKE TO TRY AGAIN.

WHAT ARE YOU? A GLUTTON FOR PUNISHMENT?

ONE LOOK AT PING MAKES ME FEEL WEAK IN THE *ARMS.*

READY... SET... *GO!*

WHAT ARE WE GOING TO DO WITH ALL THESE EXTRA DUMPLINGS?

EXTRA DUMPLINGS?

...WHERE?

Panel 1:
YOU FOUND A WAY TO WIN. I CAN RESPECT THAT.

THANKS.

Panel 2:
LOOK AT THAT. MULAN'S FIRST *MANSHAKE!*

THE STUDENT HAS BECOME THE MASTER.

End

THINKAP

TODAY I'M GONNA TELL YA ABOUT *THIS* LITTLE NUMBER.

THIS IS CALLED A *THINKAP!* Y'SEE, HUMANS DO A *LOTTA* THINKING...

SO ONCE IN A WHILE THEY WEAR ONE-A THESE TO COLLECT *AAALL* THOSE THOUGHTS FOR SAFE-KEEPIN'!

HOW YA DOIN', SWEETIE?

I NEED ANOTHER THINKAP; THIS ONE'S FULL...

End

A DISH SERVED COLD

I DON'T GET IT...

HMM?

YOU CAN'T GET MY NOSE RIGHT, EITHER?? WITH YOUR TALENT?

ARTISTIC LICENSE!

I'M SORRY I ATE THE LAST CUPCAKE, OKAY?

End

ENDINGS

BELLE?

WHAT'S WRONG?

OH...I JUST FINISHED MY BOOK.

I'M SORRY, WAS IT THAT BAD?

NO...

IT WAS THAT GOOD!

End

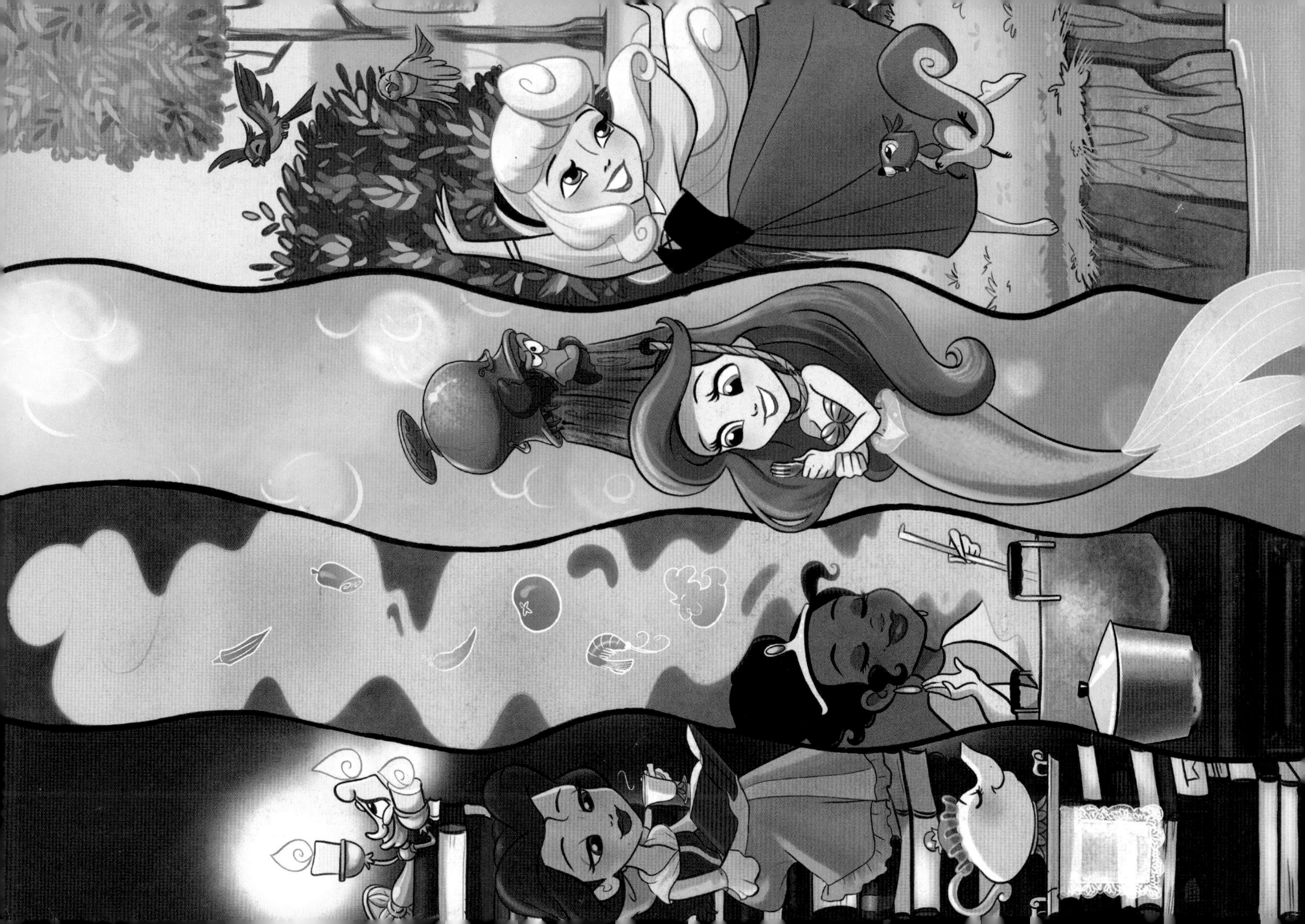

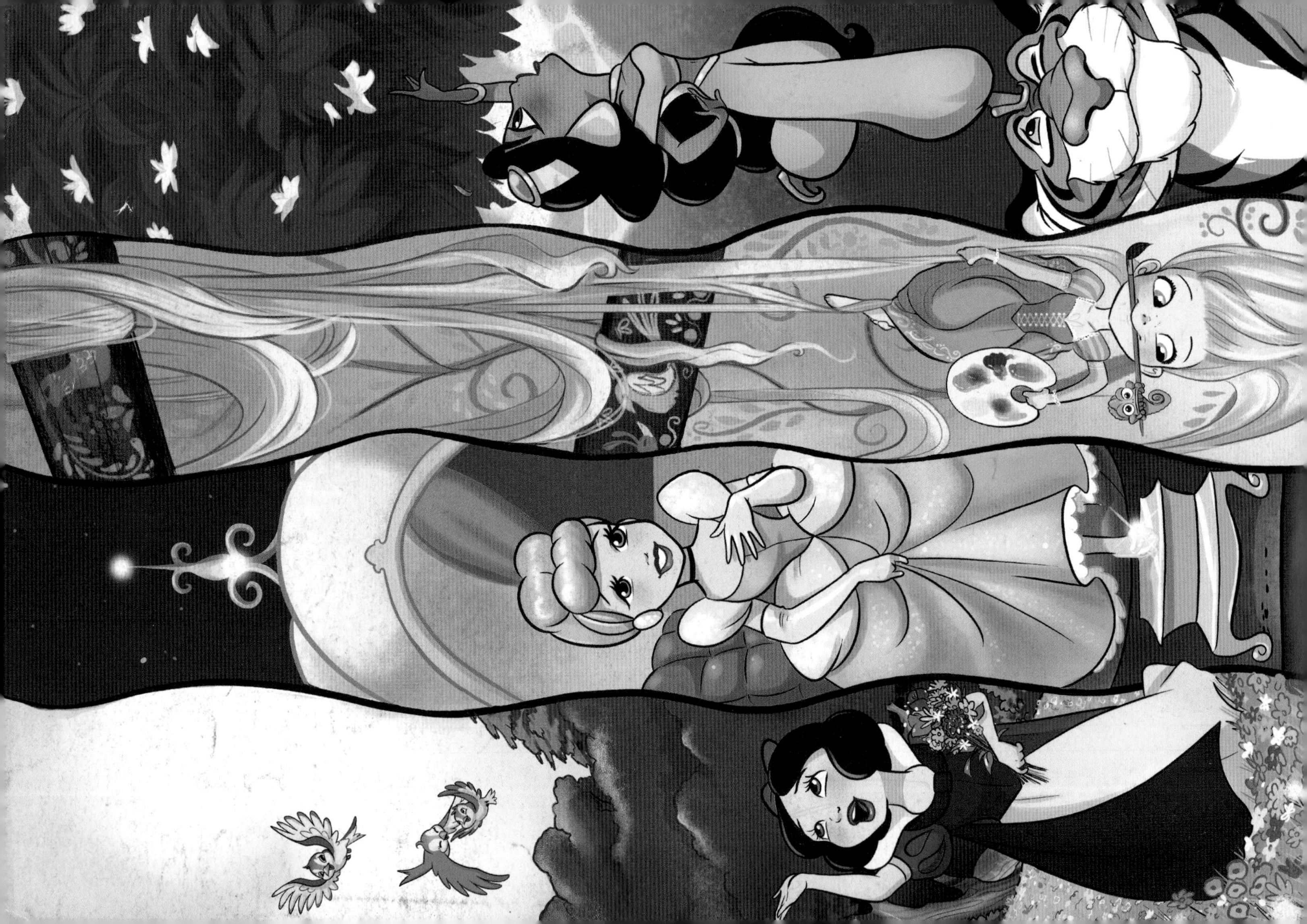

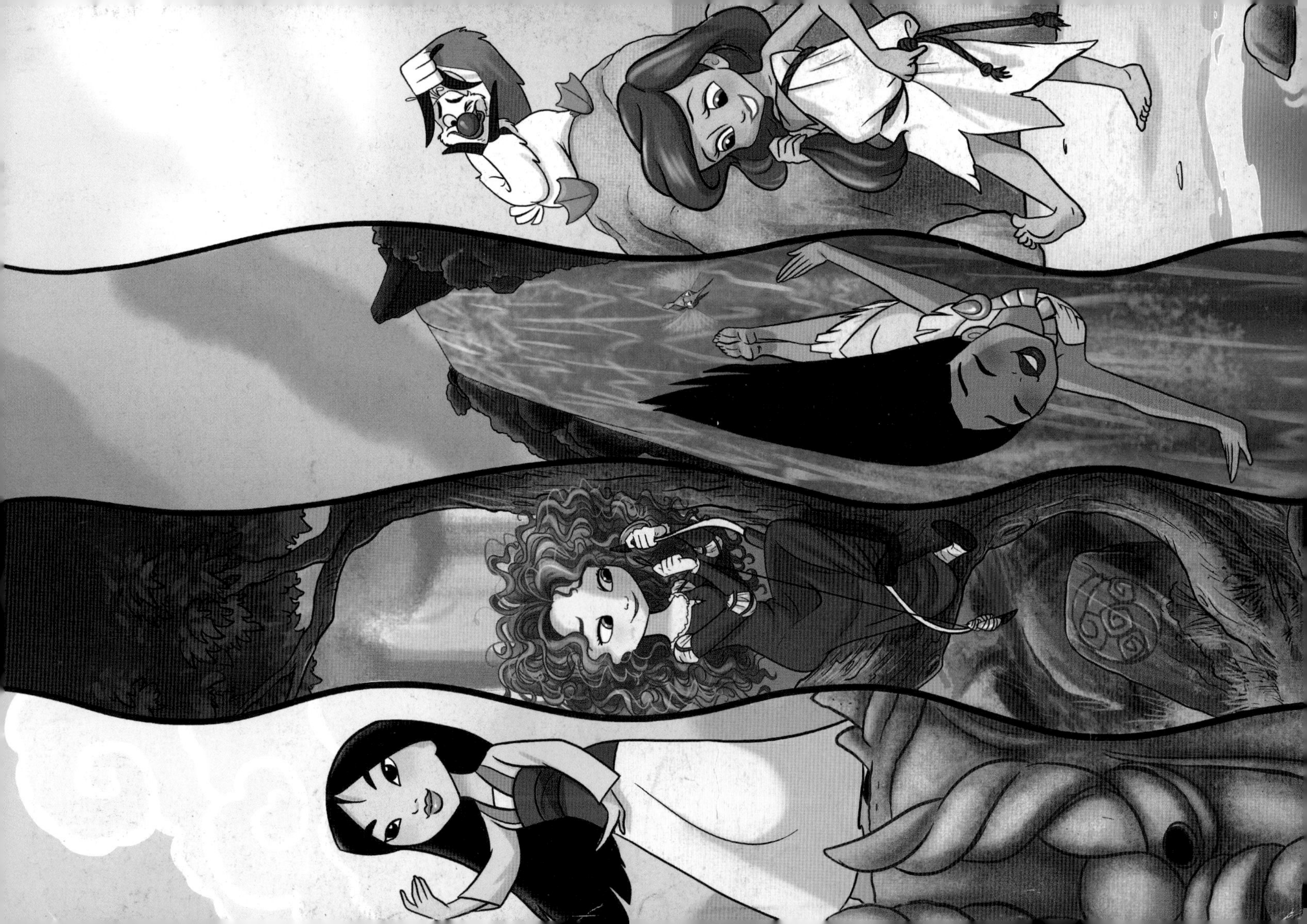

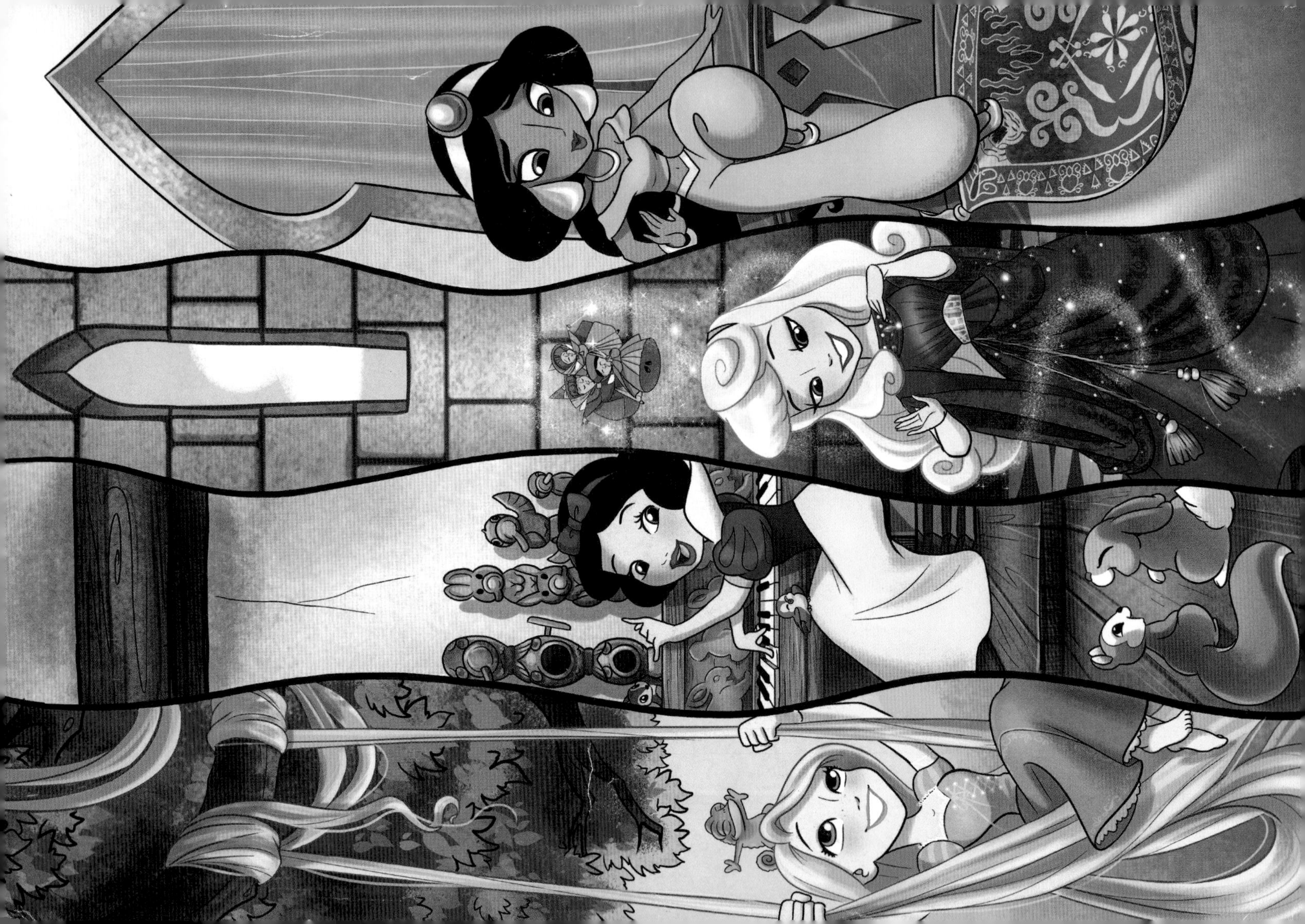